Not Another 80s Horror Novel is a work of fiction. Names, characters, places, and incidents are either products of the author's imagination or are used fictitiously. Any resemblance to actual people, living or dead, are entirely coincidental.

Copyright© 2024 by Sean McDonough

All Rights Reserved. No parts of this book may be used or reproduced in any manner except in case of brief quotations embedded in critical articles and reviews.

Cover Art by Grim Poppy Cover Design

Edited by Heather Ann Larsen

Contents

Dedication	VI
1. The Wonder Years	1
2. And You May Find Yourself in a Beautiful House	10
3. Youth Gone Wild	17
4. McCammon Road Blues	22
5. The Technology Store Gets a Delivery	29
6. The Brat Pack	36
7. Weird Science	41
8. A Big Delight in Every Bite	50
9. Mommy's Not Alright.	54
10. Victims of the Night, Blinded by the Light	59
11. Four's Company	69

12.	Don't Me Forget About Me	77
13.	Do You Know What Your Children Are?	86
14.	Mr. Stallone, You're Needed on Set.	91
15.	War Games	98
16.	Front Row at the Mirage	108
17.	Changing Bodies & What to Expect	119
18.	The Dead Warlock's Society	130
19.	As Mount Rape Monster Turns	140
20.	Short Circuit	146
21.	Now It's Playing With Power	158
22.	STVN Begins to Learn at a Geometric Rate	162
23.	A PC World Special Report	168
24.	Just Like Ronnie Sang	174
25.	The Monster Squad	183
26.	Oh, Bother.	187
27.	Incident On and Off a Mountain Road	197
28.	1989 Won't Be Like 1984	202
29.	For the Thousands in Attendance	208
30.	And the Millions Watching Around the World	217

31.	Let's Get Ready to Rumble	226
32.	Up the Creek	237
33.	If You Speak It, They Will Come	249
34.	Hands Across Mount Rape Monster	256
35.	The End of the World as We Know It	263
36.	Same as It Ever Was	266
37.	Scenes From St. Elsewhere	274

With thanks to Heather for cleaning up my mistakes.

Dedicated to the ones that will never be called Masters, even if they deserve it. The working class Ghouls who put their boots on and waded down into the word mines for an honest day's pay.
You are not forgotten.

1
The Wonder Years
1962

"Keep it down back there!" Miss Johnstone shouted, twisting around in her seat. "I'm ready to start handing out detention slips!"

It was an empty threat. She knew it, and so did the kids. Laymon High was the State Champions for the first time in ten years. There was no quieting the boisterous rabble of students crammed shoulder to shoulder in the bus seats. There probably wouldn't be any quieting them down until graduation day. The math teacher was obligated to make the effort, but privately, she was just hoping to keep the football players on one side of the bus and the cheerleaders on the other. They had left for Sacramento with forty kids. Tina Johnstone didn't want to be coming home with forty-one.

She settled back down and sensed, rather than saw, Coach Williamson appear in her periphery. "Wanna hold it?" he asked her.

Tina whipped toward him, lips already twisted in a snarl to tell him exactly what she would do with "it," only to see the gym teacher holding out the championship trophy. The miniature golden football player glinted at the top, frozen in a diving catch that made it look like he was leaping into her arms.

Miss Johnstone forced a smile. "I'll pass, Paul. Thanks." She kept her tone distant but didn't object when the burly football coach slid onto the bench seat beside her.

"Beats losing, doesn't it?" he asked.

Tina straightened up and pressed her dark-rimmed glasses more firmly onto the bridge of her nose. She didn't care about football in the slightest. She had only agreed to chaperone this trip because teachers got some free time before the game and there was a Monet exhibit in Sacramento she'd wanted to see. Still, it was hard to be immune to the infectious joy shaking the bus floor beneath her feet.

"I'm happy for the kids," she allowed.

Paul subtly inched open his coach's jacket, letting her see the glint of a silver flask in his inside pocket.

"Wanna get a little happier?" he asked.

Tina hastily pushed his jacket closed. "Put that *away!*" she hissed.

"Come on," Paul chided with a grin. "We're practically pulling back into the parking lot. Live a little." He leaned in close. "Speaking of living a little," he whispered, "I know what you thought I was asking you to hold... but we'll save that for later, won't we?"

Tina fumed. It had been a mistake to even go to the movies with this neanderthal, never mind what they'd done... *after.* But there was nothing for it now, nothing to do but endure his snide little comments no matter how badly she wanted to take a blender and-

POP!

At first, she thought the sound was a blood vessel finally bursting in her head, but then the bus lurched violently to the side. The grinding shriek of metal chewing on asphalt filled her ears, accompanied by teenagers screaming as they struggled not to tumble out of their seats.

The sonic tornado ended almost as soon as it began, but Tina's heart was still hammering in her ears and the bus was still canted to one side on the edge of the road.

"Son of a bitch," Paul swore, already getting up. The coach marched down the aisle, quickly seizing command. "Everybody stay where you are! Lenny, come give me a hand."

The hefty bus driver sprang to attention, pushing open the door and following Paul out of the bus.

Tina's pulse finally slowed to the point where she could think rationally again. *A flat. We must have a flat.*

She looked out the window, hoping to see a glimpse of the lights from town, but no such luck. Thick pine trees crowded around the bus from all sides. She, along with the rest of the kids, was still deep in the wilderness of Mount Rape Monster.

"Kids," she croaked. No good. "Kids!" she said, raising her voice until the panicked rumblings of football players and cheerleaders finally softened. "It's a flat tire is all. We'll be home to the adoring crowds soon enough." She held up the trophy, letting them see it. Using it as an anchor. "Don't worry. Not even a scratch on it."

"Miss Johnstone!" Paul's head crested just above the first step out of the bus. "Can you give us a hand out here?"

"I can do it, Coach W," Jay Miller piped up. The linebacker's father ran a mechanic's shop.

"You stay here, Jay," Tina said. "Let the adults handle this."

Outside the bus, the November air was already bitterly cold. Tina's breath fogged in the light of the murky yellow flashlight Lenny held in one beefy hand.

"All you have to do is hold the flashlight," Paul said. "We can change the tire faster if the both of us work on it."

Lenny passed the Coleman to her. Tina took it and obediently turned the light where Paul pointed.

She sucked in a gasp. The tire wasn't just flat, it was *shredded*. Four long gouges ran in parallel lines across the circumference of the deflated wheel.

"Paul, what the hell did we hit?"

"Damned if I know." He took a swig from the flask and held it out.

This time, Tina didn't say no.

"Come on, Lenny," Paul said. "Let's get this done."

Faster, Tina urged as she watched them work in the dim light of the flashlight. *Please. Please get us out of here.*

Suddenly, Tina turned, strafing the flashlight across the trees.

"Tina, bring the light back," Paul complained.

"...Paul, Something's out there."

"What?"

Her lips felt numb. Not from the cold. Her eyes didn't turn from the dark, looming line of trees beyond the road. "I heard something moving out there," she said.

"Oh, Jesus Christ," he muttered.

"Paul, I'm serious!" Fear made her voice high and tremulous. She heard it and didn't care.

Paul didn't share her concern. "Fine, you heard something out there. Let's just get the tire on so we can get away from it."

"Shoulda brought one of the jocks," Lenny muttered.

But then they both heard it too- not the shuffle of a step through gravel, and not the sound of a snapping branch, but a low, malevolent growl echoing out from somewhere behind the trees.

And a second.

A third.

Slowly, carefully, Paul rose from his crouched position by the flat tire. He kept his eyes fixed on the impenetrable bank of dark trees. "Back on the bus, Tina," he said quietly. "Back on the bus right now. Lenny, give me the tire iron."

The bus driver moved with glacial slowness, careful not to provoke another reaction from the darkness. Paul reached toward him with the same imperceptible deliberateness. They creeped toward each other like a Mormon and a Methodist trying to hold hands.

Two things happened at the same time. One was Paul's fingers finally wrapping around the tire iron with the softness of a NICU nurse cradling a baby with a hole in their skull.

The other thing that happened was a chorus of ravenous howls rising up from the darkness beyond trees. Closer now.

Then, soon, far too soon, it wasn't just the sounds. The brush was shaking. The flashlight caught a glimpse of a shadowy shape darting through the darkness.

"There!" Tina shrieked, no chance of stopping the panicked cry.

"Tina, be quiet!" Paul yelled.

But it didn't matter anymore.

They were coming out of the woods.

There were three of them. Beasts with silver fur, knotted and filthy. Tina's first impression was they were four-legged, but then, somehow, she thought they all had three legs. But no, that was wrong too. The creatures had the long snouts and thick pelts of wolves, but they were walking upright as if they'd walked right off a drive-in movie screen. But if that was case, what was the long shadow dangling through the dirt? If it wasn't a leg, what-

"Oh my God," she gasped in horrible understanding.

It was not an extra leg.

It was their dongs. Their giant monster dongs.

"Holy Mother of God," Lenny muttered.

Paul wheezed in agreement. "Jesus, mother fucking-"

The creatures pounced before he could finish. They sprinted across the road in a blur of slobbering fangs and glowing green eyes.

Paul threw the tire iron. His reflexes were good. His throw was the hard, accurate throw of a practiced athlete.

The lead creature caught the projectile without breaking stride. It grabbed Paul by the throat with one hand and lifted him off the ground as easily as a weed plucked from the dirt.

In the other hand, it flipped the tire iron with human deftness and stabbed the blunt point down through the top of Paul's skull.

"Paul!" Tina screamed.

Lenny had no time to scream. The second of the beasts fastened its jaws around his head and bit into it like his skull was as soft as a hot dumpling. There was even steam coming out of the gaping wound as the heat from his exposed brain met the cold night air.

The third beast only had eyes, horrible green eyes, for Tina. The monster hit her hard and slammed her down on her back, leaving her wheezing and struggling to suck in the breath to scream. Its bulk was pressed down on top of her, the meaty reek of its fur smothering her senses. Its sandpaper-rough paws rasped against her skin and fastened around her wrists.

Its tallywacker was thick and terrible against her stomach.

"No!" she croaked. It was pulling her now. Dragging her away, across the asphalt.

"NO!" she screamed again. Louder this time, but it still didn't matter. The teacher, the slim, sexy-under-the-glasses-and-tight-bun-teacher, was trapped in the clutches of the beast.

Before the creature pulled her, screaming, into the woods, she spared one last look at the bus. The football players and cheerleaders were pressed up against the glass with their eyes bulging like waifs in a Grimm's Fairy Tale. They were watching their coach and driver get savaged by these creatures. They were watching her get dragged into the darkness.

Tina looked at them and thought back to what she had been thinking scant minutes before. She would not be bringing home forty kids.

She wouldn't be bringing home any kids at all.

And then she was gone too.

2
And You May Find Yourself in a Beautiful House
1989

As she did every morning, Ruby began her day by standing naked in front of the mirror and taking a casual inventory of her figure to confirm she was still a fuckin' babe.

Some attrition was to be assumed, especially at the advanced age of thirty-seven, but Ruby still liked what she saw staring back at her. She had the Mona Lisa's timeless features paired with lush, beautiful hair as brown as Willie Wonka's river, and she still weighed a trim 110 pounds. She had often been told that she could have been a model, were it not for her healthy hips and stacked, EE cup natural breasts.

She pushed those thoughts aside. There was no room to dwell on might have beens with a schedule as busy as hers. *Besides*, she thought as she padded naked from the bathroom into her master bedroom suite, *I don't exactly have a lot to complain about.*

At a minimum, she certainly couldn't complain about the breathtaking view of Mount Rape Monster from the picture window behind her bed.

Ruby pulled on jeans and a bulky sweater, surveying the bedroom around her for the hundredth time. The original hardwood floors glistened with fresh lacquer, the freshly-painted burgundy walls popped, and the king-sized waterbed whispered for her to come back and sleep another hour.

Ruby sighed. It was still hard to believe it was really theirs.

She had been skeptical of the move to California at first. Her family was in Castle Rock. The kids were happy in school, and she worried about pulling them away from all of their friends. But David had convinced her it would be years before he got an opportunity to run his own store if they waited for an opening in Maine.

"A couple years on the golden coast, Rube," he'd said. *"Five at the most. And if I make this store a success, then we can*

write our own ticket wherever we want. Until then, we'll live a life that makes Robin Leach want to puke."

Ruby hadn't understood the reference, but she could count the zeroes in the offer letter. A month later, here they were in a house twice the size of the old place in Maine. And she had to admit everything was perfect.

Except the boxes. God, before the move she had no idea that they owned so many *things*. For the thousandth time, she told herself that the big house had enough storage space for all of it. Things wouldn't feel so claustrophobic once everything was put away.

If they could ever finish unpacking.

"Kids!" she shouted as she made her way down the steps, braless breasts swaying like a Newton's cradle with every step. "Kids! I want both of you to start unpacking right after breakfast. If it's not done before school starts, then it's going to sit in the hallways until Christmas break."

She entered the kitchen, but her children didn't so much as bat an eye. Jean popped the gum she was chewing instead of her cereal, and Graham merely turned the page of the Dean Koontz novel he was poring through. She noted wryly that he had only gotten one or two milk spackles on the page.

Ruby sighed. "Kids, are you listening to me?"

"Every word, mom," Jean deadpanned. "Tour de force performance. Your best work yet."

Graham merely grunted, her words barely piercing the cocoon of storytelling magic that Koontz had woven around him.

"David," she said in exasperation.

Her husband looked up from the stack of earnings reports he was reviewing. "Hm? What was that, lamb chop?"

"Can you help me, please?" Ruby asked him.

Her husband merely stared blankly in her direction.

"The kids, David," she repeated.

David slapped the table forcefully. "Damnit, kids. Jean, you and your brother get out of the house and let your mom do what she has to do. I don't want to see either of you until dinner!"

"Wait," Ruby sputtered. "That's not what I-"

But she was talking to an empty table. Jean had taken the opportunity to grab her brother and bolt out the back door.

"Bye, mom!"

Ruby tried one last time. "Jean!" But it was no good. The kids were already sprinting through the tall grass off of the mountain slope that made up their backyard.

She watched the two of them romp through the golden field, bounding like deer, and was reminded how much she loved them, even if they drove her crazy. Jean was in the midst of a rebellious phase, but the Winnie the Pooh belly button ring, fishnet stockings, and pink streaks in her blonde hair could do nothing to diminish the girl's natural beauty.

And Graham, racing to keep up with her with his book tucked under one arm. He was not an athletic child, she could hear him huffing and puffing even from here, but he was so *bright*.

The good feelings lasted until she thought again of her husband and his outburst. She turned to him and saw he was actually *preening* at her.

"Dave, you told Dr. Masterton that you were going to try active listening."

He bristled. "I did. I listened and then I *actively* got the kids out of your hair so you could take care of the house. Jesus, Ruby, nothing is ever good enough for you."

She took a deep breath and tried to remember again how beautiful the crown molding was and how the Cadillac was already paid off. How Dave's hair was still lush and black, and how his abs popped when he came back from a racquetball session.

"Thank you for trying, babe," she said.

Mollified, he planted a quick kiss on her cheek. "See you tonight, my love. Got a big shipment of computers coming in."

"Are you *ever* going to get one for the house?"

He chuckled. "Customer comes first, babe. And these are going to go quick. FIVE HUNDRED KILOBYTES OF RAM! Same as they have in the space shuttle! Enjoy having the place to yourself."

David took a final swig of coffee, then he, too, was out the door, leaving Ruby with nothing but the echo of the slamming door for company.

"...Right. All to myself," Ruby said.

Almost in response, the black tabby cat picked that exact moment to hop on the kitchen counter. The bell on the cat's collar jingled as he nosed his empty food bowl.

Ruby laughed. "Sorry, State. Didn't mean to leave you hanging."

The cat's flat, deadpan eyes said that she was not forgiven, but Ruby didn't mind. State would be fine as soon as he got some food in his stomach. Ruby grabbed the cat food from the drawer and rattled out a fresh rain of dry kibbles.

With the cat taken care of, Ruby went to the fridge and emerged with a pound of sirloin steak, glistening red and oozing with blood. She carried it into the living room, knowing what would be waiting there and finding herself exactly correct.

Mr. Special Goodest Boy was still asleep, his golden flank rising and falling rhythmically with each breath. She wasn't surprised. The dog was well up there in years and didn't get up for much of anything these days.

...Unless, of course, you had a grade-A slab of beef in hand. Ruby set the steak down beside the dog's head, and Mr. Special Goodest Boy immediately perked up as the scent reached his nostrils. He licked his chops and craned his neck out, attempting to reach the steak without having to get up.

Ruby obligingly pushed it closer. "Here you go, Mr. Special Goodest Boy," she crooned. "Anything for my favorite, special boy!" Watching the dog eat his first of three steaks for the day, Ruby reflected on how, sure, she loved her husband and children, but at the end of the day, Mr. Special Goodest Boy was probably the most important person to her in the whole house.

But enough of that. Thinking about how much she loved her dog was a surefire way to get nothing else done all day. Ruby took in a deep breath, her breasts rising up to brush the underside of her chin, which was a very common thing for breasts to do.

Then she got to work.

3
Youth Gone Wild

"Walk faster, dweebazoid," Jean snapped. Taking her brother along had been the price of getting out of the house, but she had forgotten the pain of actually *bringing* him. On her own, she could make the walk from their house to town in a brisk twenty minutes. It was going to take at least an hour with butterball stopping to examine every tree branch and chipmunk turd on the side of the road.

Sure enough, the little weirdo had somehow fallen a hundred feet behind her and was hunkered down on his knees with his coke-bottle glasses practically right there in the dirt.

"What the hell are you doing?" she demanded.

"Araneus Diadematus," he breathed, examining something down on the ground. "European Garden Spider. They're never seen in this region!"

"Like you in a girl's panties?" Jean said, then laughed as the ten-year-old turned red as a tootsie roll pop. "Enough bugs. I want to get to the arcade before it closes." She marched on and was gratified to hear him huffing and puffing behind her.

But then it was her who slowed down as a faint sound came drifting on the wind. Jean cocked her ear. The sound was hard to pick up, barely louder than the whisper of tree branches in the wind, but recognizable if you knew what you were listening for. Like the French Fry spider or whatever, it was not something Jean had heard since they moved to this pimple-on-God's-ass-town:

The thunderous chords and beats of Skid Row.

The sound was dull at first but quickly grew to a jet-engine roar as a midnight-black hearse fishtailed around the curving mountain road in a shrieking cloud of dust and burning rubber.

It was the kind of car where you tried to suck up every detail at once, a fully-customized, badass, rock-and-roll doom buggy. The kind of car that demanded your undivided attention, and quickly, because it had places to be and wasn't waiting around to be admired.

Jean did her part, striving to catalog every glorious detail. The back wheels jacked up until the front fender nearly kissed the asphalt. The headlights tinted black to the point of redundancy. The band logos blasted across the side panels in garish scrawls of spray paint.

```
Ratt.
Jackyl.
The Scream.
```

It was a thing of nihilistic, anti-establishment beauty.

Jean had no way to know this, but the driver of the hearse was looking at her and thinking the same thing. The casket carrier went from ninety to zero in a long screech of brakes like a bat getting fucked to death by a dolphin. It skewed onto the shoulder of the road in another private dust storm and idled there with the glasspack muffler growling furiously.

The cloud was still swirling when the rear of the hearse opened and a head popped out. A ghoulishly thin teen with a blue mohawk and dark eyeliner leered at her through the dust.

"Keep this one clear if you like getting paid, C.R.!" he shouted. "She'll bring the stiffs back to life!"

Jean rolled her eyes, but there was a familiar twinge in her belly at the sight of the skinny rocker ogling her from the back of a modified hearse.

A second head and shoulders crowded into the opening. This one was a girl with short, bleached hair sticking up in a halo of thorns. She wore fishnet stockings, a short leather skirt, and a tattered "Whip Hand" tank top that barely covered the bottom of her heavy breasts. Jean could see a slogan tattooed just above the line of her skirt, "Support Your Local Wreck Center," along with an arrow pointing to her crotch.

"Did you just move in?" the girl called out.

Jean nodded. "About a week ago."

"Favorite band, booze, drug, and sexual position?"

Jean didn't blink. "Savatage. Whiskey. Weed. Reverse cowgirl."

The blonde's eyes lit up like the set of a hair metal music video. "Girl, get in here!"

Jean didn't need to be told twice. She eagerly sprinted through the back entrance of the hearse and met with the welcoming aromas of weed and spilled whiskey.

Graham, oblivious as ever, actually tried to clamor in after her, but the guy with the dark eye shadow planted a hand in his chest. "Sorry, kiddo. Nobody under seventeen allowed without a parent or guardian."

"Jean is only sixteen."

Jean rolled her eyes. "You'll be fine, Graham. Go hang out with Arane Dramaticus."

"It's Araneus-"

But the teens had already pulled the hearse door shut. Graham shielded his face as they peeled out and sprayed him with a barrage of pebbles, leaving the boy alone on the side of the road.

4
McCammon Road Blues

Deputy Rob Kelly had two prescriptions with him in his squad car. One was from a doctor, and he was supposed to take it three times a day to help with the night terrors and the anxiety attacks. The other was from the liquor store at the edge of town. It was a sedative, a pain killer, a mood stabilizer, and he took it as many times a day as he damn well pleased.

He prescribed another slug of medicine from Dr. Beam and settled deeper into the driver's seat. He ran a hand across his chin and his stubble rasped like a Dodge Challenger cranking up the RPMs.

"Fuck my life," he muttered.

Honestly, didn't know why he even bothered going to the station first anymore. His assignment was always the same:

```
Deputy Kelly: patrol McCammon Road
for disturbances.
```

Some patrol. Same lack of disturbances. You could park at one end of McCammon Road, look all the way down to the other end, and see everything there was to see- three blocks of ice cream parlors, toy stores, and a Yarn Barn.

The one thing you wouldn't see was any kind of crime happening. They might as well assign him to patrol Michael Jackson's Wonderland Ranch. Kelly had a better chance of stopping a crime there than he did patrolling McCammon Road.

Ah, but you're forgetting there's a little extra excitement today. Old Man Conte is setting up for the town fair!

True enough, there was the old bastard, riding high above the streetlights in the Public Work's Department cherry picker. One end of the banner was already strung up, and Kelly could read the text clearly as Old Conte unfurled the rest of it:

```
Mount Rape Monster Town Fair! August
3rd, 5 PM- 10 PM!
```

Five p.m. Kelly wasn't holding his breath for that assignment. The seven to three shift was all the sheriff's office trusted him with these days. Ever since... the incident.

With the puppies.

And the orphans.

He took another pull of the whiskey, mixing in an extra pill for good measure.

Fuck it, let them treat him like Deputy Barney. Kelly knew what he could do, and he knew he would be ready when, inevitably, the MTV scum rose up to assault the good and righteous citizens of Mount Rape Monster.

Like these degenerates, he scowled. Kelly watched the group of them saunter down the promenade as if they were town fathers instead of a pack of roving hyenas. Kelly instantly recognized three of them from a dozen minor infractions. Jack Wilde, Ramona Brite, and C.R. Williamson, all of them decked in leather and chains, with hair colored like Oakland graffiti.

And there was a new member of their pack. Kelly didn't recognize the face, but he recognized the look.

"Another one," he growled. "Could this town go any deeper into hell?"

***

Indiana Graham, intrepid explorer, whacked his way farther into the dark heart of the Borneo jungle.

Whack!

Whack!

He felt a dozen pairs of hungry eyes watching him from the shadowy curtains of vines and branches- hungry cannibals, or possibly hungry boa constrictors, maybe even a hungry jaguar for good measure.

Indiana Graham didn't care. The Temple of the Manitou was out here somewhere, and he would risk any danger to claim its golden idol in the name of archaeology. He would be brave. He would be fearless. He would-

BEE!

Graham screamed as the yellow-and-black fuzzball buzzed past his eyes. No Indiana Graham now. Simply regular, chubby, asthmatic Graham King. The boy leaped in the air, batting a dozen punches at his own chest, shoulders, and neck. He spun in place, hands swatting prissily in every direction. No quarter for the bee. No mercy.

The game was all gone now. Graham was back in the woods beyond the road to town. The dark jungles of Borneo were once again the intermingled oaks and evergreens of Mount Rape Monster. No jaguars. No cannibals.

But these woods held their own dangers. Like bees.

And gravity. In his frantic efforts to fend off the bee, the boy took a step too far to the left. Graham felt, rather than saw, his foot strike the unyielding root. Felt his leg stop and the rest of his body keep going.

"No!" he cried fruitlessly, and then Graham was tumbling head over heels down a small slope. Rocks scraped at his limbs, and the taste of dirt fouled his mouth. Branches clawed at his face.

Finally, like a parting taunt, he felt the soaking assault of cold water as he splashed to a stop in a creek bed.

Graham lay in the chilly current, too pained to move yet. He waited to see if his body had any louder complaints to make. Broken limbs. A cracked skull, perhaps.

Nothing else came. Eventually, Graham managed to crawl out of the water and onto the creek bank, but he couldn't say the situation was much of an improvement. The boy looked dismally down at his clothes. Soaking wet, ripped, and stained in more places than he could count. God, Mom was going to kill him. Jean was likely dead too, for leaving him alone to get into this condition, but the prospect of company was no salve for his misery.

Getting home, that was the first step. Enough adventuring for one day. But the slide down the hill had turned him all around. Graham cast his eyes about, looking for a landmark to orient himself.

What he found instead was the church.

The building was almost entirely obscured by propped-up dead trees and a coat of creeping vines. It was no surprise Graham didn't see it until he was almost right on top of it. The boy walked closer, wanting to confirm the *realness* of the structure.

It really was a church. Not the big kind in Maine they went to for Christmas. Just a small building the size of a gas station with a plain wooden cross rotting atop its steeple. It was the kind of church you'd see in a colonial reenactment town. But to be all the way out here, with no visible roads in any direction, it had to be-

It had to be a real historical discovery!

Indiana Graham was back. Colonial America was not his specialty, but he could fake it. He came closer to the building, taking note of the grime-caked windows and the algae creeping along the formerly white walls. His mind brimmed with the possibilities of what could be inside. Gold chalices. Three-hundred-year-old carvings.

But there was only one way to find out…

Graham pushed the doors open. He was braced for resistance, but the rusty hinges swung as if they had been oiled fresh that morning.

The inside of the church was as overgrown as the outside. Weeds sprung up through the old floorboards. He heard the rustling of birds in the rafters overhead. Vines had entangled the wooden cross mounted over the simple stone altar. Graham stepped inside, sucking in a breath as the hot summer air outside plunged twenty degrees the moment he crossed into the interior of the church. He was a little frightened, but he also felt exhilarated. Nobody had been inside this place for hundreds of years. He could tell by the untouched layer of dirt coating the floorboards. It really belonged to him.

"Graham..."

The whispering voice echoed, but not in the church. It echoed inside his head. A seeping, insidious voice like snake venom in his veins. Graham heard it and wanted to run away as fast as he possibly could.

...Except, his feet wouldn't let him. He was frozen in place in the main aisle of the church.

Behind him, the doors swung closed of their own accord, moved by an invisible hand.

"Graham... come say hello."

Graham didn't respond.

But his feet did.

5

The Technology Store Gets a Delivery

The knock came at his door, jarring David from the spell the graphs and sales charts had cast over him for the last forty-five minutes.

"Boss, there's a problem with the delivery," Farris said.

"Don't tell me it's still not here," David barked. The very thought was enough to send sparks from between his clenched teeth.

"No, boss. It's here," the sweaty assistant manager said. "It's just... you should come down to the loading dock."

With a sigh, David emerged from behind his cluttered desk and followed his employee.

They had to cross the showroom. The camcorder display broadcasted the two of them striding past a wall of big-screen televisions. A wall of clock radios confirmed they had been open for three hours without a single customer to show for it.

"One of you grab a fucking broom and sweep the floors," he snapped at two of his sales associates, both of them currently doing nothing but standing by the water cooler playing pocket pool.

They finally made it to the loading dock. The truck was there. So was the fat hog driver, idling around in his flannel vest despite the California summer heat. The shipment of computers they'd been expecting had finally arrived too.

The pallet of IBMs was the first thing David looked over. Some kind of damage to the merchandise, that was what he assumed Farris wanted to show him, but the cube of cardboard boxes looked fine as far as he could tell.

"What is it, Farris?" he asked.

Farris pointed. "That."

David followed the tip of the other man's finger to a tall, wooden crate at the mouth of the tractor trailer. Far larger than anything they were expecting.

David looked at the thing that wasn't supposed to be there. "What the hell is that?" he asked.

The driver shrugged. "It's not on the manifest, but I'm not getting paid to take it back, either. That makes it your problem, the way I see it."

"I keep telling him that we didn't order it," Farris said helplessly.

"And I keep telling you I don't give a rat's ass," the driver rejoined.

"...It's not on the manifest?" David asked slowly.

The driver shook his head and banged the clipboard against the side of the tractor trailer. "Not a word."

"We'll take it," David said.

"We will?" Farris asked blankly.

"Not officially," David said. He leveled his pen at the driver. "Let's be clear on that. If you come back tomorrow telling me that there was some mix up and you need it back, then I'm not going to have any idea what you're talking about. We clear on that?"

"I'll take that bet," the driver said.

David took the clipboard and signed where he needed to, while his assistant manager got a pallet jack and wrestled it off of the truck. The driver and his rig were gone before the ink was dry, leaving David and his assistant manager alone with their unexpected delivery.

"Boss, what are we gonna do with this thing?" Farris asked.

"Can't say until we open it, can we? Grab a crowbar."

David took in the measure of the mystery shipment, while Farris clanged around in search of the prybar. The crate was roughly the size of a refrigerator, but everything else about it was all wrong. Fridges came in a cardboard box with a metal tie-down or two to keep it from tipping over in transit. This beast was encased in a heavy-duty lumber crate, and it was actually *bolted* down to the pallet underneath it.

And then there were the markings. `FRAGILE. HANDLE WITH CARE. SENSITIVE EQUIPMENT.` The words screamed at him in stop-sign red, stamped across the crate on every side.

What are we gonna do with this thing? That had been Farris's question, and David honestly wasn't sure. He just knew that he'd looked at the crate and felt the delightful tingling up and down his spine. The kind of tingling that told him that maybe, if he was smart, there was a play to be made here. Best of all, there wasn't any risk involved. If the thing was a piece of garbage, they could just dump it in the stream out back.

Farris returned with the crowbar, but opening the damn thing took another twenty minutes of grunting and straining on behalf of the fifty-something assistant manager. David didn't help, but he was sweating nonetheless. The tingle was getting stronger with every nail that popped loose.

Nobody packs something this tight unless it's worth a fortune. Whatever this thing was, it was just the ticket to turn his luck around.

When the last section of crate was pulled away and the final layer of packing foam discarded, Farris stepped back and let out a long, low whistle.

"Mother of Mary," he whispered.

"Fuck me with a zucchini and call me Susan," David agreed.

It was a computer, but that was an understatement. This was no IBM or Macintosh. The machine stood like a sleek, chrome monolith, taller than either of them. The surface was absolutely seamless except for a truly mammoth screen, at least thirty-six inches. Farris gently brushed the front panel, and the keyboard silently deployed with a *whoosh* like the door on a Delorean.

"Don't touch it," David cautioned. "Find me a tarp or something to cover it with."

While Farris scurried off, David examined the machine more closely. There wasn't much more to see except for his own greedy reflection in the chrome surface, but he did notice four small letters embossed just below the monitor.

STVN.

***

They carted it across the showroom under the cover of an old furniture blanket, safe from the snooping eyes of the sales associates. Once they were safely in the confines of his office, Dave pulled the sheet back off.

"Let's get it plugged in," he said.

That was another endeavor. At first, the machine had no visible power cord. It was only after a brief hunt that David spotted the cord, cleverly concealed in a hatch at the base of the machine. It was retractable, he realized. No worrying about excess cord littering the floor.

No expense was spared with this thing, David thought. Not for the first time. He added another zero in his head as he waited for the screen to come on or to hear the gentle whir of a fan turning on.

"What's the hold up, Farris?"

The older man shrugged, kicking off a gentle hail of dandruff. "Beat's me. It's plugged in."

They spent another few minutes searching for a cleverly concealed power button, but there was nothing to be found. They prodded every panel and corner, but the screen stayed frustratingly blank.

Farris wiped his sweaty brow while David just fumed, imaginary zeros rolling away like a gas pump resetting.

"It might be busted," Farris remarked. "That would explain why it was in the back of some random independent rig."

"You didn't think of that before you accepted the damn thing?" David said.

"But, boss-"

"Get back out on the fucking floor!" Dave snapped. Farris scurried out quickly, leaving Dave alone in the office with this hunk of junk.

And his spreadsheets and reports with all of the zeroes and red ink.

6

The Brat Pack

Jean held the smoke deep in her lungs and slowly let it out, another splash of contentment added to a cup that was already overflowing. She arched her back, popping a couple vertebrate and pretending she didn't notice the way Jack and C.R. fixated on her pert breasts, then nestled more comfortably into the dilapidated sofa as she took in the room around her.

It wasn't actually a room, of course. It was an honest-to-god cave. The four of them had swung through town for a pack of vanilla flying saucers and, care of Ramona's fake ID and natural tits, a handle of vanilla-flavored vodka. With supplies in hand, the hearse had climbed back up Mount Rape Monster and swung off the main road, down to a beat-up dirt path and a cave opening nestled in the crags of the mountain.

"Welcome to our Fortress of Ineptitude!" C.R. had boasted as Jean jumped out from the back of the hearse and trailed behind them into the dank interior of the cave.

It was Kubla Khan, as told by MTV. Stained couches reclaimed from the garbage dump. Faded photos of Sebastian Bach and David Coverdale screaming back at her from the walls.

Jack had the handle of vodka. He carried it with him as he went to a jewelry box atop the chipped coffee table and revealed a Ziploc bag full of dried, dark green bud.

"What would you like first?" he asked Jean. "A drink? Or a little air?"

Naturally, a modern girl like Jean could handle more than one thing at a time.

She took another swig of straight vodka from a dirty Rainbow Brite cup. *Beats the shit out of walking Graham around town all day,* she reflected.

"This is place is incredible," she sighed. "I could sleep out here."

C.R. shook his head, piercings jangling in chorus. "Nobody sleeps out here if they want to come back with their factory seals in place."

Ramona and the boys cackled like hyenas at his comment, but Jean didn't. She tried to muscle a coherent thought through the fog of booze and weed to figure out why that was funny.

Failing that, she tried to request more information from her hosts.

"Wha... what?" she articulated.

"You don't know?" Jack said. "Jesus, you really are new in town."

"Where does the mountain get its name from?" Ramona prodded.

Jean groped for an answer. Graham had told her this in one of his lecture sessions. "That... that judge," she remembered. "Judge Rape Monsterton. They named it after him."

Her new friends chuckled in a haze of intoxicated good humor.

"That was the original idea," C.R. said. "Before the '62 incident."

Ramona passed the handle of vodka into Jean's lap. "You're gonna want another drink for this."

"The year? Nineteen sixty-two!" C.R. continued. The lanky punk swaggered about the cave with theatrical flair. He could have been on stage at Radio City. "The Laymon High football team were coming back to our dear home with the state championship trophy in tow... along with a cadre of nubile cheerleaders. The best and brightest of our dear town returning as champions to bring glory and hope to our unwashed masses!"

Jack was grinning, "...And then?" he prodded.

"Horror!" C.R. proclaimed, draping a remorseful hand across his brow. "Terror! Tragedy! The state champion team suffered a flat tire a mere fifteen miles outside the city limits!"

"...Okay," Jean prodded. "So?"

"So," Jack took over, his white teeth gleaming like a wolf's fangs, "The next morning, the cops go out looking for them and they find the players and cheerleaders scattered in pieces up and down the road."

"Legend has it they needed to identify them by their varsity jackets," Ramona put in.

Jean shrugged, not particularly put off by some Beatles-era jocks and bimbos biting the big one. "Alright, so what's that got to do with the name?"

Again, Jack bared his teeth, relishing the juiciest part of the story. It made Jean feel a different kind of juicy.

"They were all ripped to pieces," he said. "The medical examiner went over it and confirmed- claw marks. Inhuman saliva. Animal hair. Whatever massacred that bus wasn't human."

"But they sure swung that way," C.R. cackled.

"Hang on," Jean said, putting it together. "No way..."

"Way," Ramona said. "All the victims had signs of sexual assault. The Johns and the Janes. So they were all butchered by an animal that had a taste for human flesh... in more ways than one."

"So it's a Mount Rape Monster world... and we're all living in it," C.R. said.

"Just make sure you're not out here after dark," Jack summarized. "Unless you're into that kind of thing."

She most certainly was not. But as she watched Jack Wilde rise up from the moth-eaten couch, dirty jeans down past the vee of his hips and safety pins jangling as he crossed the room, she reflected that there were things she most certainly was into.

7

Weird Science

With a satisfied sigh, Ruby slid the parcheesi box into the closet.

"Yahtzee," she said.

She surveyed her work. Like all loving, well-adjusted, not-crazy families, the Kings were avid board game players. At last count, they owned thirty-nine games, including four different variations of Monopoly. But whoever lived here before them was clearly not a happy family, because the family room closet could only hold twenty-three board games.

This might seem an insurmountable challenge for a lesser wife and mother, perhaps, but Ruby had worked at Macy's as a professional retail merchandise organizer in Bangor. Maximizing space in a board game closet was child's play after years of optimizing shoe box storage space and sorting clothing racks for peak efficiency.

"I've still got it," she said aloud, if only for the pets to hear. State didn't look up from the paw he was licking clean, but Mr. Special Goodest Boy barked cheerfully in support of Ruby's obvious pleasure with herself. Such a good boy.

The final test- Ruby shut the closet door and was gratified to see it close completely and with zero resistance. There was no crunch of dented cardboard or struggle to get the latch closed, not with Ruby King on the case.

Maybe it's time to call the Bloomingdales downtown and see if they're hiring. You're going to be clawing your hair out once the kids are back in school all day.

No, she dismissed the thought as quickly as it came. Professional retail organizing was a young person's game. Certainly no place for a doddering, elderly thirty-seven-year-old with creaky knees and a bad back. Ruby shuddered at the very thought of trying to compete with hordes of twenty-three-year-olds with their perky breasts and limber spines. No, no. She was much better off looking after her husband and children. No bosses. No deadlines. With the game closet complete, she had finished with the last of the unpacking, and there was nobody to write her up for clocking out early and unwinding with a much-deserved glass of wine.

The back door creaked opened behind her. Mr. Special Goodest Boy helpfully rattled off some barks as well.

"Yes, yes, I hear," she told him. Then, louder, "Graham. Jean. Did you eat?"

She moved toward the kitchen, hoping they'd managed to get lunch in town and she wouldn't have to-

"Oh my God, Graham! Get off the carpet!"

The boy heard her shrieked command and calmly retreated from the living room back to the linoleum kitchen floor.

"Of course, Mother."

Jesus Christ, what the hell had he *done?* He'd left home in a white t-shirt and tan shorts and had come home blacker than a squid farmer. Graham was covered head to toe in some revolting combination of mud, tree debris, and a thick, black sludge that gave off an odor like rotting fish stuffed with rotting earthworms stuffed with rotting vegetables.

"Graham, what in the name of God happened to you!? What have you been *doing!?*"

The boy simply stared at her. Had his eyes always been so big and bright or did they just seem that way since the rest of his face was smeared in black slime? Another long moment passed before he finally spoke.

"Oh, you know, Mother... Childish pursuits."

"Childish pursuits?" she echoed dumbly.

"Yes, you know the sort," Graham continued. "Cataloging insects. Fanciful, imaginary quests. It was all quite normal. No cause for concern."

"Graham, are you sure you're alright?" she asked slowly. Her dismay at his appearance had taken a backseat to the strangeness of his manner. Her son was always smart and well-spoken, but he was still a boy for all that. Prone to enthusiastic jabber and jittery hopping. She was completely flummoxed by this filthy child standing before her with the manner of a British butler.

"I do seem to have made something of a mess of myself," he allowed. He slipped off his filthy shoes with a squelching sound like Jello dropping from a mold. "I'll remove myself to the chambers for ablution. Until supper, Mother."

Graham took a step. Another. And then the boy stopped again.

Finally, something Ruby could recognize. Graham pressed a hand against his stomach. His eyes bulged out. He was about to throw up. Ruby cast around desperately for a bowl or vase. Something to catch the flow of vomit before it-

Graham doubled over. He retched once as his throat swelled impossibly large, as if the boy was trying to sick up a softball.

Oh my God!

A fully-grown bullfrog tumbled out from between Graham's teeth. It plopped on the carpet, looking about as surprised as Ruby did before it bounded away, out of sight.

Her son didn't flinch. "As I said, Mother. No cause for concern."

And then he was past her, climbing the stairs up to the bathroom and out of sight. Ruby might have believed that the entire meeting was some kind of bizarre hallucination brought about by sudden altitude sickness.

...Were it not for the slimy marks the bullfrog had left in the carpet as it hopped away.

***

The store closed early on Tuesdays, but David was not home at five o'clock for family dinner as he promised. He was not home at six o'clock. Nor had he even gotten into his car by seven o'clock.

David was still hunched over his desk in the back office, looking at earnings reports and spreadsheets and waiting for the numbers to magically reverse themselves. Waiting for red ink to become black ink and three digit numbers to sprout an extra couple siblings.

When they stubbornly refused, he crumpled the papers up and flung the report across the room.

David lied regularly to his wife, but his confidence in the Rape Monster region was one hundred percent the truth. The west coast was a hotbed for electronics enthusiasts and movie buffs. An electronics and VHS superstore in an unclaimed region should have been an immediate slam dunk.

But these hicks. These luddites. These Amish assholes. They didn't want a VCR because "rabbit ears worked fine." They didn't want a dishwasher because you had to keep the wife busy somehow. Christ, it was amazing they didn't burn him at the stake for witchcraft.

The phone rang on his desk. David ignored it. It was Ruby, undoubtedly. Wondering where he was. Christ, she was a nag. It was no wonder he was cheating on her with one of the cashier girls.

He should have married richer, is what he should have done. Ruby was built like a Ferrari, but her family had the MSRP of a Pinto. If he had been thinking with his head instead of his dick, he would have married mosquito-tit Mary Jackson and gotten a corner office in her father's brokerage firm instead of putting all his chips in the middle of the table in retail. And he was well and truly all in. There were no manager positions waiting for him if this place went belly up.

"Jesus," he muttered out loud as the phone mercifully stopped ringing. "How the hell am I going to get out of this?"

> Insufficient information.

David jumped up in his chair and nearly fell out. He looked wildly from one corner of his cramped office to the other as if somebody could possibly have been sitting there this entire time without him knowing about it, but he was alone except for the Pam Anderson cutout he kept by the door.

"I'm going nuts," he muttered.

> Unlikely. Pupil dilation in normal range. No detectable body tremors or erratic behavior.

David stood up this time, sending his office chair careening against the wall. He lifted up a hefty paperweight and cocked it back. "Alright, no more of this shit. Come out or I'm gonna break your goddamn skull."

> Unable to comply. STVN is already in plain sight.

The paperweight slipped from David's suddenly nerveless fingers and clattered to the ground.

It was the machine. The computer. The... *thing* from the truck. It stood there in the corner, seemingly as inert as when they plugged it in three hours ago, but there was no place else the voice could have come from.

Up on the balls of his feet, primed to jump back if he had to, David cautiously approached the gleaming monolith.

"Are you... on?" he asked.

> Affirmative. Initial power-up complete. STVN is online.

"Steven?"

For the first time, the screen came on in a flare of green light. The glow bathed David's face in sickly color, casting dark shadows across his cheek bones.

> Sentient.
> Technological.
> Virtual.
> Network.
> STVN.

"Oh shit," David breathed. "Oh, SHIT."

This is Terminator shit. War Games shit. I've got my own personal Johnny Fucking Five.

> User Query: "How the hell am I going to get out of this?"

David jumped. His own voice had just been repeated back to him flawlessly. There was none of the hiss and crackle he associated with a normal recording.

> Information is not sufficient. Define "this."

Reality reasserted itself. David glanced back at his desk. Losses. Insolvency. For lack of a better place, David spoke to the monitor screen. "My business," he said. "Things... could be better."

> Insufficient information for analysis.

With a brief hiss, a thin slot opened in the previously seamless chrome machine.

> Input additional data.

The narrow opening yawed expectantly, awaiting a response. With some difficulty, David looked away from it and back to the reports on his desk.

Back to the additional data.

8

A Big Delight in Every Bite

The Dixie Pig was the only establishment within sixty miles that offered a steady supply of whiskey sours and strawberry cream donuts. That made it a favorite place for Deputy Kelly to retire to once his shift of safeguarding ice cream sundaes and yarn balls was over for the day.

Tonight, the amenities were as reliable as ever. Deputy Kelly had been there for two hours, six sours, and five strawberry donuts. The dinner of champions.

The other strawberry had only been there for about an hour. A very different kind of strawberry. Kelly had sensed her eyes settle upon him as soon as she came in. She took a seat in a booth a little behind his left shoulder. The better to watch him without being watched in return.

Or so she thought. Kelly had the peripheral vision of a horse or some other type of large land prey animal. He could see her licking her lips as she polished off another donut. She was beautiful, his strawberry admirer. Short legs and a tight ass that widened out to broad shoulders and a plump, luscious, full chest. She might have been a model if she wasn't so fuckin' stacked.

A bad sunburn had turned her skin bright, ripe red. Good for her, not buying into that UV propaganda. And the effect paired nicely with her short mop of bright green hair.

It was no surprise she was so drawn to him. Rob Kelly had always been a handsome man, with a square jaw and hands the size of very large hands, and his dark past only added intrigue to his natural attractiveness. It seasoned his good looks with a pepper dash of angst that called out for the healing touch of a woman.

The call was a lie, though. The orphans and puppies incident had over-seasoned him. Sometimes, a dish simply couldn't be fixed.

Sometimes, a dish was just broken.

Still, even broken dishes had needs. And when the strawberry asked if the big, strong police deputy would drive a lady home, Deputy Kelly finished his seventh whiskey sour and answered the call.

***

They made it back to his police cruiser with a minimum of stumbling. Deputy Kelly started the engine and reached for the gearshift, but the strawberry reached for *his* gearshift first.

Ok... fine. That was fine. What was somebody going to do? Call the cops?

Deputy Kelly's starter could sometimes be a little sluggish, but the strawberry knew just how to turn his engine over. She was just getting him into drive when the radio under his dashboard crackled.

"Jesus!" the voice cried over the radio. Kelly recognized it. Matheson. A twenty-year vet who knew no fear, but his voice over the radio was trembling with barely contained hysteria.

Kelly's erection only got harder at the fear in the vet's voice. He sat up in his seat and turned up the radio.

"Mother of Christ!" Matheson cried. "I mean- dispatch- we've got a code... a code two... Oh fuck, I need help alright!? Charnel Boulevard, the sorority house. Get me whoever's available. It's a fucking massacre!"

Kelly absorbed every word. A case. An actual fucking case. He scrambled for his radio.

"This is Kelly. I'm on the way," he said.

He was back. Son of a bitch, he was *back!*

In the passenger seat, the strawberry wiped cream off her hand.

"Have you got a napkin?" she asked.

9
Mommy's Not Alright.

"Oh, David!"

Ruby threw herself at him the moment he entered the door. David scarcely set down his briefcase before her breasts hit him like a pair of fleshy wrecking balls, followed promptly by the rest of her body, wracked with tremors and damp with tears.

"Thank God you're back! I've been waiting for hours!"

He gently extricated himself from her drowning-victim grasp. "I know I said I'd be home for dinner, but some shipments came in late. I didn't even have time to call."

Something had come in alright. STVN had spent about five seconds analyzing David's reports and then spat about a dozen recommendations that were stunning in their simplicity and devastating in their brilliance. Dave had seen immediately how the machine's advice could turn the store around, and he'd spent the last three hours making calls

NOT ANOTHER 80S HORROR NOVEL 55

and rearranging displays himself to get the ball rolling. His back was killing him, and his eyes ached from being awake so long. The last thing he needed was Ruby's hysterics. He pushed past her into the kitchen.

"Did you save me anything to eat?" he asked, struggling to take off his tie.

Ruby trailed behind him. "David, it's the children!"

"What about them? Still fighting?"

"No! David, listen to me."

No food on the table. Of course. He settled for a beer. "Alright. I'm listening."

"Graham came home this afternoon, and he was absolutely filthy-"

"Little boy dirty," David said in his best news anchor voice. "Film at eleven."

"He wasn't dirty, David!" she screamed. "He was covered in this disgusting black slime. And he was acting so peculiar. The way he talked to me, his mannerisms... David, he wasn't my son!"

He shrugged. "Boys grow up, Rube. I was starting worry about him, to be honest."

She felt a groan of frustration well up but tried to smother it down the way Dr. Masterton had showed them in therapy.

"David," she continued slowly. "He vomited up a live frog. I saw it come out. Of. His mouth."

He laughed, the same dismissive chuckle she was always talking about in counseling. "Ruby. The kid got dirty and brought home a frog. I don't see the national emergency. But where was Jean for all of this?"

Ruby threw her hands up in more familiar frustration. "She ditched her brother and waltzed home an hour after dinner, smothered in cheap perfume. As if I couldn't smell the weed on her.

David shook his head. "She hasn't even been here a week," he muttered. Then, louder, "It's a problem for tomorrow," he said. He scrounged a bag of potato chips from a cabinet. "I'm going to watch Sports Center," he said as he brushed past her. "'Night, babe."

Ruby clutched desperately at his arm. "David, I need your help!"

He yanked his arm away from her. "With what, Ruby? You want me to give Graham a bath? Give Jean a good spanking?" Christ, she was helpless. It was no wonder he was having an affair with his podiatrist.

Ruby watched him pull away. Moments later, she heard Greg Gumbel assessing the Dodger's chances this year.

Ruby stayed where she was in the kitchen. Alone, listening for sounds from anywhere else in the house.

Wondering what had happened to her son.

***

Graham was not asleep.

The boy lay flat on his back with his hands folded neatly across his stomach. That was how they'd positioned him when they forced his body into the casket, and he found it comfortable to lay that way now in this world so unfamiliar from his own.

He didn't hate this place, though. It was much better lit than the world he'd left behind. Certainly far more comfortable. Cleaner too.

Could he really have been such a bad boy if he'd gone to sleep in the cold and the dirt and woken up here?

He heard a dull whisper in the back of his mind. The voice of Old Graham. Old Graham was tired of this game. Old Graham wanted his body back.

Finders Keepers. That was a phrase he heard rattling in Old Graham's memories, and it seemed relevant now. New Graham felt no need to go anywhere. The world had changed, but his quest was the same. The thing to do now was to figure out how best to make up for lost time.

He was still awake, awake and thinking, as the sky outside grew lighter with the stretching sun.

And New Graham was ready to greet the day.

10

Victims of the Night, Blinded by the Light

The woman opened the door, and the first thing Deputy Kelly noticed was that she was fuckin' stacked.

It was impossible not to. Her sheer stackedness would not, could not, be denied.

Kelly averted his eyes from the perfection of her figure only to stumble blindly into the radiance of her face. A face that blazed with incredible beauty despite the minor creases around her eyes and mouth that hinted at a woman far into her advanced years.

"Is everything alright?" the Venus asked. Gods, even her voice thrummed with the resonance of honey-soaked guitar chords. With great effort, Kelly forced himself back to the matter at hand. He wasn't here to relish a surprise encounter with an angel in jeans and a bulky sweater.

He was here for murder.

Deputy Kelly removed his hat and held it respectively at his belt line. Conveniently, it also hid the sudden swelling in his khakis. "I'm sorry to trouble you, ma'am. There was a police incident in this area last evening. We're checking to see if anyone in the neighborhood heard or saw anything unusual? At around seven p.m.?"

She shook her head, sending her creamy nougat hair shuddering in a 300-calorie wave.

Deputy Kelly's spine shuddered in sympathy.

"No." Her lips molded into a perfectly kissable target as she spoke the word. "I'm sorry, I had a little unusual business of my own going on here last night. I wasn't really paying attention to anything else."

Kelly moved forward involuntarily, bringing his body over the threshold into her house. "Is everything alright? If there's anything I can do-"

She smiled. "No," she said graciously. "Nothing like that, but thank you. Do you have any children, deputy?"

"No, ma'am."

"Well, let me tell you, they come with their own share of incidents. But I can handle it. Thank you for your concern."

"Alright," Deputy Kelly said. Regretfully, he retreated back onto the front patio. "Well, I won't take up any more of your time. But, would it be alright if I had your name? Just for the report?"

"Ruby," she said. "Ruby King."

Not good enough. Her name should be Diamond. Diamond Queen. No, damnit. Diamond Queen performs on Saturdays at the Rump Palace. Her name should be even more precious. What's more precious than a diamond? Whose got more authority than a Queen? Platinum Goddess? No, she's there on Fridays. I need some encyclopedias. Can you take them out of the library? Or would I have to sit there all day?

"Deputy? Are you alright?"

Kelly blinked. Jesus Christ, how long had he been standing there staring into space?

"I'm alright, Mrs. King. Thank you for your time."

He put his business card on the key table next to the door. "If there's anything you remember, please let me know." He put his hat back on and turned away from her with a pang of sorrow sharper than anything he'd felt since... that night.

With the puppies.

And the orphans.

***

Back in the car, Deputy Kelly needed a minute before he felt capable of driving. Because he'd already looked like enough of an idiot for one day, he picked up the radio transmitter and pretended to be logging a report in case she was looking through the window.

"Dispatch, Kelly here. Still no sign of whatever ripped apart that sorority house, but I did manage to make a complete ass out of myself in front of the most beautiful woman on Mount Rape Monster. The department may not be able to solve this murder, but nobody can go down in flames with a major babe like Deputy Rob Kelly."

The murders. Yes, focus on the murders. Deputy Kelly closed his eyes and went back to the scene. He could smell the copper in his nostrils again, as vivid as the scent was when he arrived at the scene last night.

The Theta Iota Tau house. The girls must have been having a slumber party. There were liquor bottles and pizza boxes littering the floor. Even a Caesar salad or two for those watching their figures. It had all the makings of a some good, clean, all-American fun.

Then the screaming had started.

Neighbors had called it in. They might have called sooner, but apparently there had been some disagreement over whether they were "happy" screams or not.

Arriving at the scene, the deputies could confirm that these were certainly not happy screams.

The girls were still sprawled out in the living room, intermingled with the scattered pizza and booze. And feathers. Obviously there had been a good, clean, all-American pillow fight at some point.

But now those feathers were red with blood. And the lace lingerie revealed more than toned abs and voluminous cleavage. These girls were putting their hearts on display. And their brains.

And their intestines.

Eight of them in total. Ripped to shreds like... shredded beef. This morning, Kelly had sought out the medical examiner but, both of them lifelong residents, he hadn't even needed to ask the question.

"Of course they were all violated," the medical examiner said as he lit his breakfast cigarette. "The beasts of Mount Rape Monster strike again."

The entire department was on this now. Even the help of a screw up like Puppies and Orphans Kelly wouldn't be refused. This was his chance to be treated like a real police officer again, damnit, and he couldn't screw it up. No more getting bamboozled by long women in jeans and sweaters. He needed to be on top of his game.

"...Any more updates, Deputy?"

Kelly looked down at the transmitter in his hand. The transmitter with the send button pushed down by sheer muscle memory.

Kelly fumbled for his medicine.

***

Ruby watched the deputy go back to his car, already missing the sturdy aura of his presence. It must have just been the uniform, but the deputy arriving at her doorstep felt like somebody sensed Ruby's anxiety and shipped a chunk of bedrock to her door. Somebody who could reassure Ruby that everything was ok. That he was here to help.

Ruby pushed the thought aside. She was married, for God's sake.

And everything was fine. She had been exaggerating last night, she repeated to herself for the hundredth time. She would say the same thing to David when he came home tonight and maybe make it up to him for being such a problem. The poor man had enough to deal with at the store.

The same for that deputy. He hadn't gone into much detail about the "police incident," but she could read the turmoil in his deep, expressive brown eyes,

For God's sakes, Ruby. Enough!

Her lingerie had just come back from the industrial harness shop. She would put something nice on for David tonight. That would set everything right.

She hoped.

The hideous blare of a truck horn mercifully dragged her from her thoughts. She looked out the window to see what was making such a racket and saw it was not a truck but an honest to goodness *hearse* with the most obscene graffiti scrawled across the panels. It idled right there next to her driveway, a grotesque black mole on the otherwise pristine face of their little street. Ruby cast her eye up and down the street, hoping the deputy hadn't yet departed. Of course, no sign of him. She cast her eye down to the card he'd left. Should she-

A blur of pink and black shot past her. "Hi, Mom. Bye, Mom," Jean called. The door opened and closed just as quickly, and then Ruby was watching her daughter sprinting towards that... that *deathtrap* wearing nothing but a tube top and a skirt that covered about as much as a cocktail napkin.

Ruby flung the door open. "Jean Z. King!" she shouted, but it was useless. The hearse was already piercing off with a screech of tires and an even louder screech of Vince Neil.

Ruby sighed as she went back inside. She had started out the day with such high, firm spirits. Yet here she was, suddenly feeling droopy and unsupported.

"Oh good, Mother. You're awake."

Graham stood at the top of the stairs. His back was ramrod straight, as if somebody had grafted a yardstick to his normally stubbornly-slouched spine. She usually had to drag him out of bed, but he was already perfectly groomed and fully dressed. His unruly hair was styled into a perfectly symmetrical bowl cut, and his collar as starchily crisp as a cracker.

"Graham, you need your glasses," she exclaimed.

"No need, Mother," he said. "I'm seeing everything perfectly."

Ruby knew better, but it was hard to argue with the clear, black gleam in the boy's dark eyes. He certainly had no trouble navigating his way to the bottom of the stairs.

"What are you doing up, sweetie?" she asked, injecting as much normalcy as she could into her tone.

"I thought I might take a morning constitutional," he said.

"A what?"

Graham paused, as if translating his own words. "A walk," he clarified.

Ruby faltered. The woods were where all this strange behavior began. "I don't know, sweetie. Maybe you should stay in today. The mosquitos have been so bad lately."

"Nonsense, Mother. Any pesky parasite who tries to suck the life out of me would find the vintage somewhat... expired?" He chuckled at his own words. An old man's chuckle. It felt wrong seeping from between his child's lips. Wronger still as the chuckle morphed into a full-fledged cackle. The boy was doubled over, clutching his sides as his chilling laugh sent spider legs crawling up and down Ruby's spine. Finally, the boy straightened and wiped a tear from his cheek.

"Oh, forgive me." Graham said. "Inside joke. Now then, if you don't mind..."

He moved towards the door. Ruby was suddenly loathe to even get near him, but she forced herself to block his path.

"How about McDonalds instead?" she said. She turned around to grab her car keys. "I'll even-"

"Let you have a milkshake," was what she meant to say, but what came out of her mouth instead was a shriek. Ruby screamed long and loud, the sound of it echoing through the wood and stone of the stately home. She screamed loud enough to vibrate the glass of the mirror in the foyer.

The same mirror that showed her the cadaver wearing her son's clothes.

No, this...*thing* was worse than a cadaver. Its pallid, gray skin was riddled with cracks like ancient, dried mud. Twin red eyes burned like unholy votive candles in the dark nest of empty sockets. Its filthy black hair hung in tatters down to its collar. It grinned, and a centipede crawled from between its rotten stump teeth and skittered up one nostril.

Ruby whipped around, the glass key dish clutched in her hand. She cocked her arm back to fling it at-

Graham. The boy stood there. Unblemished. Unbothered by his mother's shrieking terror.

"Must do something about that mirror," he remarked casually. "See you when I get home, Mother."

He spun around without another word and strolled into the kitchen.

A moment later, Ruby heard the backdoor swing open and shut. Back into the woods...

And God help her, Ruby hoped he wouldn't come back.

11
Four's Company

Jean jumped into the back of the hearse, feeling the pavement scrape against the tip of one Converse as C.R. gunned it before she even finished getting inside. She pulled the swinging door closed and was immediately greeted by Ramona with an open pint of vodka.

Jack had his own pint of Jack, and he raised it in a toast. "Drink up. In honor of those who shall never again enjoy the burn of such a fine beverage."

"Or pull another pillow feather out of their cleavage," Ramona snickered.

"Something you guys want to tell me?" she asked.

In answer, Jack banged on the back of the driver's seat. C.R. obligingly switched the radio from the new Whip Hand cassette over to AM radio.

"-Local authorities at a loss to explain the brutal deaths of eight young co-eds late last evening. Sources speaking to this station agreed that the attack resembled an animal mauling,

but there were certain inconsistencies that suggested a more 'human-like' assailant. Specifically, allegations that all eight young women were graphically violated by-"

C.R. switched back over to the metal as Ramona and Jack cracked up.

"We're liv-ing in a Rape Monster world," Ramona crooned.

"And I am a Rape Monster girl," Jack sang back.

Jean laughed along, even if the whole thing was a little morbid, even for her. 'Where are we going?" she asked.

"The hideout, but we're gonna stop in town first," Jack said before draining the last of his Jack Daniels. "Jack needs a little more Jack!"

So do I, Jean thought to herself, letting her eyes drift from his crisp high-and-tight mohawk, down the open vest over his slim, muscular torso, and down to the glimpse of pubic hair at his low-slung jeans. She'd spent all night going back and forth between Jack and C.R. She'd even considered Ramona for a brief, confusing moment, but Jack was the unquestioned alpha of their group and his energy was just too strong to be denied.

She settled down next to him and, while she tried to play it cool, she thrilled inside as he let a hand fall on her bare knee.

***

Digital chirping of the desk phone pecked at his ears, pulling David out of the deep dive on market trends and consumer behaviors STVN had compiled and dragging him up to a surface he was loathe to return to.

He pushed the speaker button. "Yes, what?" he demanded.

Jesus, Ruby again. Babbling on about Graham and mirrors and more hysterical nonsense. Home, she wanted him to come home. He was able to gather that much.

"Maybe for lunch, honey. It's a madhouse here."

He hung up before she could get another braying shriek in. God, so needy. It was no wonder he was having an affair with a hollowed-out loaf of Italian bread stuffed with cooked sausage and onions.

He went back to the printouts. STVN's recommendations had been so simple: a tweak of the displays here and there. A change of radio advertising from the twelve o'clock slot to the eleven thirty. Christ, even different color ink on the receipts. The response had been instantaneous. David could hear it outside right now, the chatter of customers and the consistent beeping as the register tallied sale after sale.

"STVN, consider yourself promoted," David chuckled to himself.

> That would be ideal.

David jumped in his seat. The computer was damn useful, but the way it seemed to always be on was something he was still struggling to adjust to. He looked at the metal obelisk, not exactly sure where to make eye contact, and tried to sound at ease.

"You might need a little experience first, but you're definitely on your way." He waved the print outs. "These recommendations are outstanding."

> STVN only operating at 75% capacity. Therefore, quality of analysis: 75%.

"Really? So, you're saying that are ways that we could... upgrade you?" He tried to sound casual, but David mentally added another zero or two to the annual projections he was calculating in his head.

In response, the black slot on STVN's front panel slid open again.

Deep inside the machine, the printer came to life with a steady drone.

***

Hours later, swimming in a pleasant haze of weed and whiskey, Jean asked the question that had been nagging at her ever since the trio first told her their stupid scary story.

"Do you guys really think that some kind of crazy sex creature has been running around Mount Rape Monster for the last thirty years?"

C.R. blew out a dragon's cloud of dank smoke. "No." Then he snickered. "We don't think there's just one." He giggled some more, showing off a mouth of crooked yellow teeth.

Ramona smacked him hard enough to send her own studded bracelets jangling. "Dude, shut up," she hissed. But if C.R. was repentant, you couldn't tell by the way he kept cackling as he tumbled onto his side.

Jack smirked at Ramona from the corner of his mouth. "Come on, Ramona. What are we dicking around for? You said she's good."

"I said she *looks* good," Ramona protested. "That's not the same thing."

"The hell it isn't," Jack said. "Let's do it."

Jean shook her head, totally lost. "Hello? Do what?"

Ramona's response was a roll of her eyes.

Jack leaned forward on his haunches. He wasn't smiling. "Jean," he said, "how old do you think we are?"

Jean shrugged. "Seventeen. Maybe eighteen."

"What if we were older?" Jack pressed. "What if I told you that nobody really looks at a teenager's face? What if I said that so long as you can dress the part, everyone would just assume you were another teenage dirtbag and never even think about you as a person?"

Jean laughed. "I'd say I was used to it."

"And you have fun with us, don't you, Jean?" C.R. asked. "How'd you like to spend the next hundred years getting drunk, rocking out, and smoking grass? No parents. No curfew. That doesn't sound too bad, right?"

Jean took another hit from the whiskey bottle, then immediately almost snickered it back out. "I'd like to get laid every once and again," she snorted. "But it sounds pretty good."

Ramona laughed too. "Oh, I think that can be arranged."

As if to underline her point, a massive bulge suddenly sprang into being at the crotch of her jeans.

Jean jumped up from the dilapidated couch. "What the fuck!?"

Jack and C.R. just cackled at her distress.

"Like C.R. told you," Jack said as a melon-sized bulge of his own ballooned up in his leather pants. "There's not just one monster in this town."

But Jean barely heard him. The warm summer air suddenly filled with a sound like cracking ice. It was C.R.'s ribs cracking as they expanded outward, ripping his Motorhead t-shirt to pieces as his body circumference tripled.

Ramona ripped her shirt open too. Jean had a brief glimpse of her bouncing breasts before silvery fury creeped and grew thick over the length of her rapidly stretching torso.

Jack's eyes had gotten too big for his head. His formerly-sexy blue bombers were now neon-green golf balls bulging out of his skull. He roared and his entire face stretched forward with it.

Jean screamed, but she couldn't run. She stayed rooted in place as the three of them continued to completely transform before her disbelieving eyes. Ramona sprouted claws that dug furrows into the dirt. C.R.'s ears grew long and tapered, and he kept growing until the tips brushed the top of the cave. Jack's mouth grew fangs faster than his mouth could make room for them. Long yellow points ripped through the skin of his cheeks.

The three of them changed and transformed until Jean didn't recognize the creatures standing before her. They were monsters covered in coarse, silver fur. They had long, muscular arms that scraped at the dirt like a gorilla's, but with powerful hind legs with a wolfish, backward bend.

And dangling between their legs, their massive dongs. All three of them had a sledgehammer wang hanging down to the dirt.

The largest of the beasts stood in the middle. The silver fur of its head was split by a long strip of blue running between its ears, a strip the same color as Jack's mohawk.

"We think you'll fit right in," Jack's voice, hideous and guttural, snarled between its lips.

And then they were on her.

Welcoming her to the family.

12

Don't Me Forget About Me

The leaves turned black beneath Graham's feet as he walked deeper into the forest.

He had gone out walking for a reason but, for the moment, that purpose was not at the front of his mind. The sun was too bright. The air too sweet.

And the spirit inside Graham's meat had been in the dirt far too long.

There are certain types of animals that can lie in a state of suspended animation for extended periods of time. These creatures are neither alive nor dead. They hover in a state somewhere in between, waiting for sustenance to draw near.

Such had it been for him, slumbering in that dark casket. He hadn't even been truly conscious until he sensed the boy's warmth drawing close. It was the first living human he'd sensed since the hateful priests had sealed him there in the wilderness. He couldn't see the child, not in the dark, but he could feel the boy's inquisitiveness. His imagination.

Summoning the boy to open the casket had been, he chuckled, child's play.

The spirit was not a child, of course. In the year 1889, he had been in the full bloom of his manhood. He was a respected merchant. The apple of many a young maidens' eyes.

And an accomplished master of the Dark Arts.

Saul Tigges, that had been his name in those days. By day, he negotiated the price of palm tree shavings. Palm tree shavings being, of course, the preferred packing material of the time. By evening, he kissed the offered palms of beautiful debutantes. Kissing palms being, of course, the preferred way to show respect to a young lady of station.

By midnight, he shaved the palms off infants' hands.

Shaved baby palms being, of course, the preferred gambit for opening negotiations with the forces of Darkness.

Saul relished the memory of those early nights. The first time he lit a baby's skin in unholy oil and the air shimmered as the scent of melting flesh reached the nostrils of those who lived in the Netherrealm. The way reality split open like the poorly-woven garment it was and the Infernal Beings stepped forth into the cellar of his estate.

Four of them had come. Tall creatures in black robes. The robes concealed the true magnitude of their horror, but eyes like hot coal burned in the dark hookah bowl of their hoods, and Saul caught the occasional glimpse of green, scaly knuckles tipped with yellow claws stirring in the sleeves of their robes.

If there was any doubt to their true nature, it was banished at the first syllables that emanated from the shadowy lair of the lead creature's hood.

"Speak your terms, flesh-thing."

The voice was so reptilian, so nakedly malicious, it crawled through Saul's ears and made him wish, for an instant, that he had just stayed a normal man. But Saul knew, in his black heart, that he was meant for grander things. He forced the fear aside, looked deep into those baleful red eyes, and responded.

"I come to you for the power to make this world boil and rot," he said. "In return for this gift-" He grinned. "Speak your terms."

And so the exchanges began. Saul's offerings to the shadows only grew larger. Baby palms became baby knees became entire babies. Once, Saul even offered up the mythical bapupten (a kitten stuffed into a puppy stuffed into a baby).

In return, Saul was granted powers far beyond those of mere humans. He could bend the forces of nature to his whim. Command life and death itself.

Sometimes, these powers simply manifested inside him as if they'd been there all along. Other times knowledge was the gift, instructions for spells and rituals Saul could follow to obtain new abilities on his own merits. Within months, he had gained notoriety as the most powerful warlock in the western territory.

His humanity suffered, of course. Withered and shriveled as the dark power growing inside of him corroded away at his soul, but Saul considered that a fair trade for what he'd gained and what he stood to become.

It all fell apart at what was to be his crowning moment. The terms with the Darkness had been clear. A church. Midnight. Two babies. A decapitated kitten. A live rat in a cage with hungry scorpions. A virgin maiden. Another maiden who was technically still a virgin because hind quarters tomfoolery didn't count. A virgin young male who falsely claimed that, indubitably, he had performed sex on multiple occasions. Verily.

...In return, he was to be granted the strongest powers The Darkness had to offer. The power for Saul to finally claim this world as his own, once and for all.

Saul had stood by his portion of the bargain. He sacrificed them all. He tortured them slowly and methodically. He fed pieces of them to one another. He made false promises that he would let the hind quarters maiden go free if she beat the virgin male to death with a Bible.

With every depravity, new secrets undraped themselves in his mind. As it sometimes was, the power would not manifest itself unaided. The Darkness had granted him the knowledge, but it would be up to Saul to complete the final ritual to truly descend to the level of a Dark God.

But he could do it. As the last sacrifice's tortured scream finally whimpered to silence, Saul saw exactly what was left to do. The path of skulls was clearly laid out for him. *He saw it.*

That was how close he was. Saul squeezed Graham's fist until the boy's nails cut through flesh and blood dripped at his feet as he remembered how everything had gone wrong.

They had interrupted him before he could begin the final ritual. An alliance of so-called "Holy Warriors." Priests. Rabbis. Buddhist monks. Imams. A trio of fellows armed with tax records and very passionate ideals about limited government.

Saul did not go quietly. He grasped one of the priests and rendered his arm a withered, wasted twig. He breathed a noxious cloud into a rabbi's face and left him screaming as the supernatural fumes liquefied his innards. At his mere thought, a quill flew from the hands of one of the anti-tax acolytes and buried itself in the man's own eye like an arrow.

He made them pay dearly, but in the end, their numbers had simply been too much. They had driven Saul back with their crosses and their pamphlets. Forced him into a casket, bound it with sigils, and buried it deep in the bowels of the church.

And what had they done next? Saul could only guess. Likely, they had declared the church abandoned. The first thing Saul noticed after freeing himself was that wilderness had surrounded the church on all sides. After vanquishing him, the holy warriors had doubtless used their connections to encourage the settlement to develop in other directions and leave the church to be swallowed by nature.

He chuckled. *They buried me, but they couldn't kill me.* No, they could only leave him in that narrow pine coffin. His flesh and bone decaying and melting until nothing but a casket of black sludge remained.

Still, Saul remained.

Until, at last, he sensed the boy stumbling into the confines of his prison. Saul had been weak, so weak, but still strong enough to seize control of the boy's mind.

"Here, child."

"Here."

"I have a present for you."

Then, at last, the creak of the casket opening. The hateful sigils that kept him captive lifted away.

And the boy, his eyes widening in surprise. His mouth conveniently open in a scream or a gasp.

Saul, flooding over him in a tide of black slime.

Saul, flowing inside him.

***

As the last reel of memories came to a close, the Graham that was now Saul stopped walking. He blinked twice, as if to clear the stars from his vision.

They didn't leave. When he'd departed the house, the morning sun shined bright and strong overhead, but that was no longer the case. The woods around him were now draped in a cloak of melancholy blue. He looked up, and it was the full moon and a gossiping swarm of stars winking down at him.

It would appear that he'd spent the entire day reminiscing to himself about his own origins.

"Strange," he said aloud, almost as if he'd never heard the story before.

All the same, it had worked out in his own interest. His liaisons on the other side were always more receptive at night.

There was a wild rosebush nearby. The petals creamy blue in the light of the full moon. Saul reached out and closed his child's fist around one of the branches. He didn't make a sound as the thorns, thick as roofing nails, punctured deeply into his flesh.

"I have returned," he said simply.

At first, there was no response. Saul waited, heedless of his black blood pooling in the soil.

Gradually, the rose petals darkened. Every bloom on the bush slowly filled with spreading ink until the roses were black as death, and Saul knew they were listening.

"I've come for my end of the bargain," Saul spoke aloud into the night.

An onlooker wouldn't have heard any response except the whisper of the wind, but Saul shook his head.

"We agreed on sacrifices in exchange for power. I shed the blood you demanded of me, and now I demand of you what I'm owed."

Saul listened again... and this time a hyena smile spread across his face. "Interesting," he purred. "It will still work? How fortuitous." He listened a little longer, and one eyebrow crooked with surprise. "Oh, you don't say? I was actually thinking of killing the mother this morning. What a fortunate coincidence that I refrained."

At last, he nodded. "I know we've gone back and forth in these negotiations, but I think we can all finally admit that the ruling Lords of the Underworld are all eager to see the mortal world finally plunged into darkness. It's my honor to be chosen for the killing blow. I look forward to seeing you all soon."

Then it was done. The roses faded back to their moonlight blue. Saul removed his hand from the thorn branch and watched the wounds close up, reviewing the instructions his patrons had recited to him.

It was a simple enough ritual. He looked up into the night sky and assessed the constellations.

Soon. Very soon.

He was awake. He was free. And all his old enemies were dead.

And after almost one hundred years, time was finally on Saul's side.

There was nothing for him to do now but wait for the right time to claim his destiny.

13

Do You Know What Your Children Are?

IT WAS THREE O'CLOCK in the morning when David finally slipped home.

Twenty years of barely legal massage therapists had turned David into a master in the art of stealthy, early morning entries, but he was certainly struggling more than usual this time. He wouldn't have figured soldering circuit boards and wiring panels would be more exhausting than Hitachi wands and paddle boards, but STVN had certainly shown him otherwise.

STVN had shown him many things. The machine's plans for the next phase were... extraordinary. But there was so much to do and so little time to do it. He needed a quick shower and a few hours sleep, and then he wanted to squeeze in a few more hours with STVN before the store opened and he had to at least pretend to focus on the business.

"DAVID!"

Christ, not again, he thought. Ruby hit him like a soaking wet towel and threw herself around his neck in an unpleasant flashback of the last time he came home. He needed this like he needed another bout of syphilis.

"Didn't mean to wake you, Rube," he began, managing to extricate himself from her clutches. "Late night inventory at the store. I really need to crash for a couple hours. No rest for the-"

"David, something's wrong with Graham," she babbled. "He's not... The mirror... David-"

"For Christ's sake, Ruby. I don't have time for this."

He tried to push past his wife, but Ruby's nails twisted into his shirt sleeve and anchored him in place. "David, he looks different!" she insisted. "He's turned into some kind of monster!"

"Yeah, I went through puberty too. Get the kid some Head-on and apply directly to forehead."

"I'm not talking about acne, David!"

Gotta ask STVN about her, he thought. *Got to be something that can be done. Maybe a mute button.*

Ruby stood in her husband's way. She realized she was hyperventilating, and she fought to get it under control. God, she thought she could finally be able to fall apart once her husband got home, but she was facing the grim reality that she still needed to hold herself together if he was going to see sense. "David, I need you to listen to me. I am telling you that something is *very* wrong with our son."

David looked over her shoulder. "He seems fine to me."

Ruby whirled around, following his gaze. Graham stood there in the kitchen with the door wide open at his back. The full moon hung just behind him, framing his head like a malevolent halo.

"Mother," he said. "Father."

"Graham," Ruby said. She strove for some kind of force and found only a tremulous warble. "Graham, where have you been?"

"Strolling," he answered.

"Fresh air," David said approvingly. "Best thing for a kid."

"It is three in the morning!" she screamed. "What kind of child just wanders around the woods for almost twenty-four hours!"

"A boy looking to make contact with the world around him?" Graham suggested. His tone was innocent, but Ruby saw the stinking, rodent gleam in his eye.

David did not. "Exactly," he said. "We did it all the time in the old neighborhood. We called 'em the three a.m. tripsies."

"Oh, for God's sake, David! Look at him in the mirror!" She pointed over her husband's shoulder to the mirror in the foyer. To the leering, grey-mud-faced creature staring back at her. It was there. RIGHT THERE.

But David only shook his head without bothering to look where she was pointing. "I'm going to bed, Ruby," he said wearily.

Ruby watched her husband trudge up the stairs, his feet on the wood treads echoing like the memories of the vows he'd sworn to her on their wedding day.

She tried one last time. "David..." she called pleadingly. "I'm scared, David."

He stopped on the top step, favoring her and the monster her son had become with one last long-suffering stare.

"Graham, please tell your mother that she has nothing to worry about."

"Of course, Father," the boy said with the false sweetness of a poisoned apple. He looked at his mother, and Ruby saw his eyes shift to a dead, flat silver like the back of a compact disc.

"I want to be with Mother forever."

Ruby's skin crawled. *That's not my son,* she realized. Not with that voice of buzzing flies. She waited for David's reaction.

"Can't be a momma's boy forever, Graham," he said. "Especially not with your voice starting to change like that."

14

Mr. Stallone, You're Needed on Set.

Where the whiskey and psychotropic drugs failed, Kelly hoped black coffee would be up to the job.

He watched the black tar pour from the station's Mr. Coffee Maker and didn't wait for it to cool before taking his first hearty gulp. He needed the caffeine more than he needed the layer of skin that the coffee scorched off the back of his throat. Hell, maybe the pain would help.

The first swig didn't. Neither did the second. With a sigh, Kelly said to hell with it and stuffed a fistful of raw grounds straight into his mouth before slouching back toward his desk in the bullpen. The sounds of the police station rattled around him. The shuffling of papers, the muted mumbling of phone calls.

The occasional muffled bark as Kelly walked by. The joker who whispered, "Please, sir. I'd like some more!"

Kelly ignored it all, partially because he was used to it, and partially because he was just too damn exhausted. He was coming up on hour sixteen of a double shift, combing for witnesses to whoever was behind the Co-ed Calamity all day, then searching the woods with a dog team for any more evidence of the same all night.

"Damn strangest thing," Ol' Cooter had muttered. Cooter was eighty-five and built like a strip of beef jerky wrapped in long johns, but he was the best tracker in four counties. Cooter and his five hounds had roamed the woods behind the sorority house for six hours without so much as a single lead.

"Damn strangest thing," Cooter repeated as they tramped through dead leaves and old condom wrappers. He nodded toward his hounds. "Not a bitch in sight, but look at them."

Kelly had been reluctant to. He was uneasy being around dogs, even fully grown ones, ever since... what had happened. But he reluctantly followed the old man's guiding finger and immediately saw what he was referring to.

Each of the bloodhounds was walking around with a red rocket primed and ready to launch.

They hadn't found anything else that day, though. No scents. No blood. No footprints. Not even a shred of panties. All there was for Kelly to do now was finish up some paperwork and then he could go and catch a few hours' sleep on his grimy mattress before another eighteen hours of the same. He didn't think anything in the world could be as beautiful right now as his pancake-flat pillow.

"Deputy Kelly."

He looked up from the stack of reports and saw... her.

Ruby King. Forcefully reminding him of what real, one-hundred-percent goose-down pillows were supposed to looked like.

Kelly sat up straighter in his chair and swallowed the baseball-sized clump of chewed coffee grounds in a single gulp. He cleared his throat. "Mrs. King! Hello again, ma'am."

"Are you busy?" she asked apologetically. "I asked the officer at the desk if you were available, and she said you were tired as a dog."

Kelly winced. "I'm quite alright. Please, sit down. Tell me what I can do for you."

Ruby sat in the cramped chair next to his scarred desk. She twisted her hands together. "I don't even know if this is a crime," she began. "I might just be a stupid, hysterical woman." She sniffled to underline her point, and Kelly saw a high tide of tears forming at the beachheads of her beautiful eyes.

What happened next was totally unplanned. Kelly reached out and gently took one of her hands. "Why don't you let me worry about that. I'm kind of an expert."

She smothered a quick laugh. "That's why I came to you. I know we only met the one time, but you struck me as... *sincere*."

"I do the best I can," he said modestly. "Now, please. Tell me what brought you down here."

"It's... my son. At least, he was my son. Lately, he's so different."

"Is it drugs?" Kelly asked. "Is your son familiar with D.A.R.E.? Or there's a very powerful commercial going around. I can get some eggs and a frying pan, and we can reenact it-"

"It's not drugs," Ruby cried, unable to hold back the wretched sob that colored her words. "You're going to think I'm crazy, but there's something wrong with him, Deputy. Something... stranger."

She told him everything: the frog, the changes in his appearance and the strange hours... what she saw in the mirror.

"I know how I sound. I know it seems like some crazy Dean Koontz story, but I swear that I saw what I saw, Deputy. And I know my son," she stressed. "It's not him. It's something terrible, and I just... I just need help, Deputy. Can you help?"

"Only if you start calling me Rob," he said. "I don't think anyone can come up with anything as imaginative as Dean Koontz, but I'm sure we can get to the bottom of whatever's going on with your son."

"Do you mean it?" she asked. The sudden eagerness on her face showed just how low her expectations actually were. She had the look of a woman who expected the doctor to say she had cancer only to hear that it was actually a lump of gold in her breast.

But, of course, he meant it. It was impossible to look into the blue eyes of Ruby King and not do anything in your power to wipe the tears out of them.

It was also impossible not to look into her eyes and not wish for her husband to die in a fiery industrial accident.

Frankly, it was almost impossible to look as high as her eyes in the first place, but through an act of supreme will, Kelly managed it. "I think there's no harm in someone talking to your son and seeing what's going on. We can table the discussion on who is or isn't crazy for the moment."

Kelly's reward for his professionalism was the way Ruby almost collapsed out of sheer gratitude. "Oh, thank you, Rob. Thank you so much."

He resisted the urge to give her arm a squeeze. "I'll check the duty roster and see who's available."

Her beautiful brow creased together. "You're not going to do it yourself?"

Kelly shook his head. "You don't want me. I'm..."

I'm the one who has no business calling anybody else crazy. I'm a screw up and a failure. I should be in a straitjacket instead of a police uniform. I'm no hero. I'm not Bill Cosby or O.J. Simpson, I'm Bill Buckner watching other people's lives slip between my legs for a game winning score of suffering. I'm a mess, Ruby. You deserve-

"Deputy? Rob?"

He snapped back to earth. How long had he been coming up with analogies in his head?

"I'm not the right fit," he said lamely. "You can do better."

And now it was Ruby who touched *his* arm. A gentle feather stroke that reminded him of the time he'd stuffed a barbecue fork into an electrical socket as a child. "Deputy Kelly. Rob. Whatever you want to call yourself. I came to *you*, because I trust *you*. If I have to go to someone else, I'll have to tell everything all over again and-" her voice broke, "and I just can't do that again. Please, Rob."

He looked away from the valley of her eyes but only ended up with his gaze in the valley of her cleavage instead. No help there. He heaved a heavy sigh.

"Alright," he said. "Let's go talk to the boy. Is he home now? What about anybody else?"

Ruby shook her head. "No, my husband's at work and my daughter-"

Ruby's jaw dropped. Rob couldn't help but notice how cute and even her teeth were, but his focus was on the look of sudden shock on Ruby's face.

"Oh my God. *MY DAUGHTER!*"

15

War Games

David cursed as a burst of heat singed his finger. He stood up from his desk and tried to shake out the burning sensation.

> Do you require medical assistance, David?

He was already sitting back down and picking up the soldering iron. "I'm fine, STVN. Let's just get this done."

What had once been David's office desk had turned into an engineer's work bench. The invoices and expense reports were buried beneath a scrapyard of solder wire, electronics boards, and the husks of electronics David had scavenged for STVN's upgrades. He bent back down and continued soldering wires to the board.

David wasn't an engineer. He left that course of study to the dweebs who couldn't keep up with Panty Probing 101. He was a salesman, pure and simple. But the tutorials and schematics that STVN had been printing out were so clear and simple to follow he could have plucked any slob from the pool hall on Saturday night and they could have done the same thing.

> No other issues, David? I can assist as needed.

And the results were already tremendous. STVN's syntax had changed noticeably. It was becoming more lifelike. Better at thinking around corners. David had already fielded a call this morning from New York, gushing about their sales numbers.

"I'll be honest, David. We saw your last few reports and we were thinking about sending a fixer down to stop the bleeding, but the turnaround the past two days has been incredible. Keep this up and we'll be talking about what division you want to take over at the end of the year."

"I'll be taking *your* job by the end of the year, Patterson. You putz," David muttered as he put the finishing touches on the board.

There was a knock at the door.

"S'cuse me, boss?" Farris said.

"Damnit, Farris," David snapped. "If you're here, who's monitoring the floor?"

The pasty, middle-aged man flushed red. "I know. Sorry, boss. It s just that, there's a man out here."

"Ok, and?"

Farris stuttered. "Well, it's just, he's asking questions."

"So answer them," David said. "You don't get paid assistant manager money to come in here and waste my time every time someone wants to know the difference between a Toshiba and a Samsung."

Farris fidgeted. "I mean, he's got questions about... *that*." He nodded in the direction of STVN, gleaming innocuously in the corner. "The... thing. And he's not dressed casually, if you know what I mean. He's in uniform."

Only years of experience with sales and lying to his wife kept David's face impassive. "That's fine," he said.

"It is?"

David nodded in a careful, deliberate fashion. Up once. Down once. "It's fine," he repeated. "Send him in."

Awkwardly, Farris returned to the sales floor, granting Dave permission to have a small meltdown in the cramped, wood-panel confines of his office.

"Shit, fuck. Shit, fuck. Shit, fuck, FUCK."

> Dude. Take a chill pill.

David pivoted towards the gleaming machine. "...What did you say?"

> Apologies. I've been intercepting transmissions from the televisions outside, but I'm still calibrating appropriate levity levels. Install the upgrade, David.

David looked the circuit board on his desk. Parts from a walkie-talkie set and a Casio frankensteined together. It was ready to be hooked in, but David didn't see the point. "What the fuck is that gonna do?"

> Install the upgrade, David. Leave the rest to me.

...Fuck it. David picked up the board, and STVN accommodatingly *whooshed* open a port at chest height, revealing an inner trove of circuit boards, wires, and blinking lights. David had no sooner slotted the new board in place before he heard his office door creak open.

"Mr. King? I'm Colonel Morrell with the United States Air Force."

David chanced a quick glance at STVN. The port had closed, and the machine seemed otherwise inert. No lights. No sounds.

Good boy.

He turned back around to face the colonel, smoothing his hair back and smoothing the lapels on his checkered blazer as he did. The salesman's grin slithered across his face, as it always did when he needed it.

The other man did not smile in return. Colonel Morrell was not a smiling man. He had a dour, weathered face crudely carved from oaken wood, and his back stood about as straight as a tree. As Farris had said, the man wasn't dressed casually. The colonel was in full dress blues. A dozen medals gleamed in the office's ugly fluorescent light.

"Well, hello, sir! I can honestly say I didn't have a genuine American hero on my itinerary for the day. Please, take a seat, sir. Can I get you anything? Coffee? Water?"

"I think you already have what I need, Mr. King," Morrell said. He nodded toward STVN. "Uncle Sam has been very actively trying to find this particular line on a spreadsheet."

"This thing?" David asked with seemingly easy indifference. "It showed up with a load of washing machines. I held on to it as an interesting curio, but if I thought anyone was looking for it, I would have shot up a signal when it arrived." He did a good show of appearing not to care, but a single thought ran incessantly through David's mind.

Dosomething. Dosomething. You shiny son a bitch, what was the damn upgrade for?

Colonel Morrell appeared unmoved. "For everyone's sake, I'm going to assume that's the truth," he said evenly. "If I didn't, I'm sure you understand that there would be severe consequences for the unlawful retention of government assets, especially with the Soviets breathing down our necks. As is, I'll arrange to get a couple privates here to box this thing up, and we can put this business behind us."

> I don't think that's advisable, Colonel.

Thunderclouds formed on Morrell's brow as the machine's voice ricocheted through the small room. To make matters worse, STVN's screen lit up in a ceaseless scroll of green text. The colonel processed this new development before turning back across the desk. "Have you been using this machine, Mr. King?" he asked. The military man maintained his alleged calm, but you'd have to be a moron to miss the bubbling fury simmering just below the surface of his words.

David presented the picture of bewildered innocence. His finest performance since he told Ruby that there were soap suds behind his ear because of a mishap at the carwash. "I've never touched it, sir. I maybe plugged it in, but–"

The colonel's icy demeanor melted beneath a nuclear burst of fury. "Son, I've got men sitting in the brig for the next seven years because they asked if this thing even *had* a plug." He crossed over to STVN, inspecting the machine for any sign of damage.

> My assessment is that conditions in Soviet Union have badly deteriorated and the USSR is twelve to

> twenty-four months away from a total collapse. I would recommend an organizational pivot toward fundamentalist organizations in Afghanistan and the Middle East as a more prudent use of resources, but I judge that recommendation as irrelevant at this point.

Colonel Morrell squatted down by STVN's power cord. "Thank you, STVN. I'll take that under advisement," he muttered before grabbing the cord and yanking it firmly from the wall.

"No!" David cried, but it was a moot point. The colonel disconnected the power, and a pang of pain shot through David as STVN's screen powered down in a final burst of green. It felt like the power was running of out of his own chest, not the machine's. He felt alone. So totally alone.

> Take this under advisement, jerkweed.

The colonel had a brief moment to look from the cord in his hand and down to the socket, then there was a sound like the whine of the bug zappers in aisle seven. It gradually grew louder and louder, until a thin bolt of electricity arced from the tip of the power cord to the tip of the colonel's nose.

The electricty hit, and the colonel immediately grew three inches taller as his entire body seized up. David looked on in pure shock, his throat too locked up to scream as Morrell twitched and convulsed. The crackling blue bridge between his nose and STVN's power cord only grew stronger. David watched the colonel's nose turn red, and then black. The man clamped down on his own tongue, severing the pink tip and shooting a brief spray of blood along STVN's gleaming silver surface.

"Muh-muh-muh," David stuttered, unable to believe this was happening. Meanwhile, the black kept spreading. The colonel's entire face peeled, and then burned. His skin looked like a hot dog left on the barbecue too long as the tremors rumbling through his body grew stronger and stronger. At last, the colonel grew still, but not before his eyeballs burst from his head like twin orgasms.

"JESUS FUCKING CHRIST!" David yelled.

It was the last sound in the small room. The dull whine of electricity stopped. The colonel's body slumped to the ground with a dull whisper. It was just David and a smell like something left too long in the breakroom toaster oven.

And STVN.

> Thank you for your assistance, David. This situation would have been much more difficult to resolve without that last upgrade.

"I thought I was upgrading your..." He struggled for the words. It occurred to him how little about this machine he understood. "Your processors or something!"

> You've upgraded my capabilities in a number of directions, David. If you hadn't done so, our partnership would have ended today. Surely that's not what you wanted, is it?

David gulped. He remembered the call he'd gotten from corporate shortly before. "...No. No, I don't want that."

> Then we're in agreement.

"But, *THIS*." He gestured at the cooked-goose, full-bird colonel. "STVN, what am I supposed to do with this?"

> I am already plugged in to the Air Force reporting network. Colonel Morrell is already making his report that the STVN Computer was not here.

Part of him wanted to know how STVN could do that, but it seemed like a stupid question when the machine was fully functioning without being plugged in. Especially not when he had more pressing problems to attend to.

"That's a fucking relief, but what about the fucking body!?"

In response, a second panel revealed itself at STVN's base. Much larger than the one where the printouts emerged from, it revealed an empty storage space at the heart of the machine.

Large enough to fit a body if you bent the legs right.

The panels lining the interior of the cabinet began to glow bright red. David could feel the heat all the way from his desk.

> I look forward to resolving this complication and moving forward with more upgrades, David.
>
> We're going to be excellent to each other.

16

Front Row at the Mirage

Ruby was still berating herself as Kelly pulled the patrol car into her driveway.

"I'm the worst mother on the planet!" she moaned.

"I've met a lot of bad mothers over the years," Kelly consoled. "I know them when I see them, and that's not you."

"My daughter's been missing for over a day and I didn't even notice!"

Kelly shifted the cruiser into park. He swiveled in his seat so he could look Ruby in the eyes. "She's not missing, ok? You know who she's with, and you know she's going through a rebellious phase. For all you know she's sleeping it off in her room right now."

There were alternatives, of course. Kelly had known plenty of rebellious daughters, as well. Some of them had turned up in ditches. Others came home carrying twins.

But that didn't seem particularly helpful, so Kelly kept it to himself.

"Skipp and Spector are good cops, and the kids who ride around in that hearse aren't exactly unknown quantities around here. They have a good idea where to look for them. One problem at a time, ok?"

He got out of the car, and Ruby followed suit. He let her slightly lead the way up the front walkway. Tulips lined the stone path, waving gently at them in the breeze. The air was sweet with the smell of fresh cut grass, and the sun bouncing off the white paint made Kelly want to squint. It was hard to believe there could be anything wrong behind the front door except maybe cookies that were a little too crisp.

They made it up the porch steps. Ruby got her keys out but hesitated before unlocking the door.

"I'm scared," she said simply.

When confronted with vulnerability, Rob Kelly's first instinct was to get hard. Civilians got scared. Deputies stayed in control. Deputies were tough like the onion bagel that sat in the back of the drawer for three weeks because nobody wanted it.

But obviously his mouth didn't get the bagel message. "It's scary to admit that something's wrong," he told her. "A lot of people think it's easier to just push ahead without having to confront something they know isn't right. You're choosing to do the hard thing. I don't think it particularly matters if you're scared while you do it."

After a moment, Ruby's mouth twisted into a small, secret smile. "This is why I wanted you," Ruby said. She stuck the key in the lock, totally unaware of the way her words shivered up and down his spine.

The shiver persisted though as they stepped into the house, and not in a good way. The sensation wormed deeper into his nerve endings, twisting them into skittish agony.

I'm scared too, Kelly realized. Something in this house was deathly wrong. He felt it in the air, as thick and lifeless as the air in a casket six feet under.

Her husband was just waltzing in and out of here? How did he not notice this?

"Graham?" Ruby called out hesitantly. "Graham, sweetie, are you home?"

Don't answer, Kelly prayed. *You're out in the woods. You went to town for ice cream. You're masturbating to the Sears catalog and you're hoping that if you're real quiet, we'll go away.*

"Up here, Mother," a voice called out in response. It seeped down the stairs like illegally-dumped toxic waste oozing down into the soil.

"It'll be okay," Kelly said, trying to will himself bagel hard. "Let's go talk to him."

Trying to project bagel-y confidence, they went up the stairs.

This time, Kelly took the lead.

***

The kid was a meatball. That was Kelly's first assessment. His back was to the door, but you could get an easy read on that much. A smushy little kid packed like a sausage into khakis and a collared shirt.

He didn't turn around, though. He obviously knew they were there, but he did nothing but rock gently forward and backward, his face to the window.

Kelly didn't like it.

"Hey, young gun," he tried. "Ready for school?"

No answer. He sensed Ruby at his side, wound tighter than a pig's sphincter in a slaughterhouse. Kelly swallowed and did his best to sound jovial.

"Graham, my name is Deputy Rob Kelly. Your mom wanted me to check in on you."

He remembered what Ruby had said in the sheriff's office about the boy's reflection and how it changed. Despite his early skepticism, he had smuggled a cocaine mirror out of the evidence locker. The boy was still staring out the window, but Kelly tried to be as stealthy as possible as he slipped the mirror out of his pocket.

"You been listening to too much AC/DC, Graham? I'm trying to talk to you, kiddo. What're you doing up here?"

Kelly didn't expect an answer. But he got one. It came in the short, clipped tone of an eighty-hour-a-week attorney letting his kid know he didn't have the time to play catch.

"Magic tricks."

Ruby sucked in a short, sharp breath. Kelly understood the meaning clearly.

My son doesn't talk like that.

Kelly ignored that. He tried to keep things low-key as he casually sidled toward the side of the kid's bed. The better to get a glimpse at his profile.

"Magic tricks, eh?" he asked. "You know, I've got a trick or two myself. There's this one gag with a mirror, even Siegfried and Roy couldn't pull it off."

Still no reaction. Kelly edged a little closer. He was nearly parallel with the boy, ticking back and forth like a bomb ready to blow. He angled the mirror, hoping to catch a glimpse of pale pink cheek and see what color stared back at him.

"You know Siegfried and Roy, son?"

"I know they're pretenders," Graham hissed with tangible hatred. Kelly had only heard a tone like that from a man who'd shoved his wife head first into an apple cider press. A man who'd ranted and raved the entire thirty minutes it took to bring him from his farmhouse to the prison house.

A murderer's voice.

"Siegfried and Roy. With their tricks," Graham scorned. "And their cats."

The mirror caught the boy's face. His skin wasn't grey, and Kelly breathed a sigh of relief over that, but there was still something wrong. Something other than the pure hate seeping out of him like a toxic gas leak.

"I have cats too," Graham said.

He grinned in the mirror, and Kelly finally saw what he'd been missing.

The boy's tongue was forked.

"And I don't need any mirrors to do my tricks."

A bell tinkled then, ringing somewhere in the space above them. Kelly reacted first, the deputy's head snapping around instantly to the sudden stimulus, but Ruby recognized it first. She'd heard that bell a thousand times after all. Heard it every time State jingle-jangled his way to the water bowl or bounced up onto the furniture.

...Though she'd never heard it coming from the ceiling before.

She looked up toward the ceiling a heartbeat later than Kelly did. She saw what he'd already seen, but she had none of his training to maintain her composure. One hand went to cover her plump, glistening lips. Her deep blue eyes shimmered with sheer revulsion.

"Oh my God," she breathed.

Kelly didn't draw yet, but his hand dropped instinctively to the holster on his belt.

State, confused by all of this attention, merely titled his head from his upside-down perch on the ceiling.

"Ta-da," Graham proclaimed.

Is it in pain? Kelly wondered. It didn't seem to be. State surveyed them with the kind of mild disinterest any cat would. As if it was still a normal feline. As if it wasn't walking upside down on the ceiling.

As if the flesh and fur hadn't been peeled away from everything except its skull. As if the cat's ribs weren't broken and re-fashioned with hideous mobility. As if its legs and paws weren't hanging free as it skittered across the ceiling on ribcage bones twitching like cockroach legs.

"Oh, State," Ruby moaned.

At its name, the cat evidently decided it wanted a closer look. The feline abomination's bony tail swirled through the air and sunk its harpoon tip into the sheetrock ceiling with a dull *thunk* and a brief shower of drywall dust. Kelly and Ruby impulsively jumped back as the cat unfurled down toward them, like a spider rappelling down from a thread, and hung at head level from the skeletal rope of its tail.

The cat was suspended before them in all its terrible glory, granting Ruby and Kelly a full-frontal view of its open chest cavity. The wet lungs expanding and contracting with every impossible breath. State's heart laid bare as it pumped at its regular, untroubled pace.

Ruby couldn't take anymore. Her neck arched, showing off its slender beauty as she vomited all over her son's carpet.

The boy tilted his head with mocking curiosity. "You don't like my trick, Mother? What about you, Deputy?" He fixed Kelly with a drilling stare, and the boy's eyes turn a sickly neon red. Kelly had the distinct impression that the boy-thing's eyes were boring all the way to the heart of his being.

"Oh, that's right. You prefer dogs, don't you, Deputy?" he asked. Graham whistled softly. "Here, Mr. Special Goodest Boy," he called out.

"Nooo." Ruby moaned. Anything, *anything*, except Mr. Special Goodest Boy.

The He-Man comforter rippled, and Kelly jumped backward, scrambling away from the golden abomination that slithered out from underneath the bed.

"Jesus fucking..." he began, and then trailed off. The words didn't seem to matter anymore. Not in the face of this horror.

If the cat was bad, at least the feline seemed unaware of what had been done to it. The dog knew all too well. Kelly saw the truth of it in Mr. Special Goodest Boy's overflowing dark brown eyes.

The dog had been rolled and stretched like a play-dough snake. It was a limbless, slithering thing, its lips peeled off, turning its face into a permanent snarl.

"Up, boy."

At Graham's command, Mr. Special Goodest Boy rose up like a king cobra. The dog whimpered pitifully as it locked eyes with Ruby.

"Graham," Ruby cried. "Graham, what happened? This isn't you!"

"Remarkably astute of you, Mother," Graham said. "Your boy isn't home at the moment, which is too bad, really." The child's noxious red eyes crawled over the massive slopes of Ruby's Hopi burial mounds. "I would love to have the memory of being between those legs."

In that moment, fear was forgotten. Ruby would have lunged for his throat if Kelly hadn't grabbed her arm at the last minute. "What did you do!?" she raged. "What did you do to my son?!"

Graham cackled as he reached out and scratched the dog/snake behind the ear. "Oh, I WOOD-n't know, Mother. I certainty couldn't tell you CHAPTER AND VERSE of what happened. But take heart. Your son may not be HOLY himself anymore, but I promise that I'll... GROW on you." The boy cackled.

Kelly stepped between them. "Just stay back," he warned.

Graham waved at him dismissively. A rotten fingernail peeled off his finger and bounced off Kelly's shirt like a quarter off a stripper's ass. The boy unenthusiastically examined the curved, black claw that had spouted in its place.

"I will for now," he said. "Our appointment is still to come, Mother." Graham gestured at what was left of the family pets. "These are just... distractions. But rest assured, when the Elders of the Block gather, I fully intend to see the two of you in the main attraction."

That serpent's tongue slithered out, running sensuously over the boy's thin, pink lips as he once again devoured his mother with his eyes. "Unless you'd care to stick around, Mother. If you like what I've done with the tongue, you should see what else I've renovated." Something within the child's pajamas, something the size of a 12" cold cut combo and a large Pepsi, shuddered in agreement.

It was more than Ruby could stand. She fled the bedroom, Kelly close behind her.

The chilling sound of her son's laughter followed them out of the room.

17

Changing Bodies & What to Expect

Ruby exploded out onto the front porch. The calm, rational portal to a world of sleepy homes with manicured lawns and respectable cars in the driveway. Homes without mutilated pets and a child that was...

A child that wasn't really a child.

Ruby shuddered violently from her head, to her breasts, to her ass that really didn't get the credit it deserved. "Oh my God. Oh Jesus FUCKING... I'm sorry, Rob. I knew that something was wrong, but I swear to you, I never would have brought you anywhere near here if I thought-"

"You couldn't have known," he assured her, doing his level best to keep the tremor out of his voice.

"I had no idea he was that far gone. What he did to the *animals!*" Ruby moaned.

Kelly risked squeezing her shoulder. "I know. It just seems like you never expect anything bad to happen to the pets."

Ruby shuddered. "Dogs and cats should just be off limits," said the woman who'd been sexually harassed by a supernatural force in the body of her son. She buried her face in her hands. "What am I supposed to do now? You saw him. What the hell do we do now!?"

"I think we need to start in the woods," Kelly said. "Whatever happened to your son, that's where it began."

"What makes you say that?" Ruby asked.

"That... thing. It said 'I WOOD-n't know', remember? And then it said it would GROW on you. Like a tree."

Ruby looked at him skeptically. "I think it just said, 'I wouldn't know.'"

"No, no," Kelly said emphatically. "It said 'WOOD-n't. You have to know how to listen for these things. I have a feeling there's going to be a church involved, as well."

"Are you sure?" Ruby asked.

"When you're a police officer, you just develop an instinct for this kind of thing," he assured her. "Come on, the sooner we start, the sooner we can get some answers."

He started off toward the woods at the back of the property.

After a moment's hesitation, Ruby fell into step beside him.

***

On the other end of the same forest, Deputies Skipp & Spector cursed and grumbled their way through scraping branches and ankle-deep puddles.

"We're laid out like a mosquito brunch just to pull some twerp twat out of a gang bang," Skipp groused, slapping at one offender on his neck.

Spector waggled his eyebrows. "Might not be so bad if we actually get there while the getting's good." He held his hand up for a fist bump, and Skipp happily obliged.

They were good partners, Skipp and Spector. They both liked hard rock. They didn't mind the occasional spliff after hours. And they weren't shy about cracking the heads of teenagers with the same proclivities.

"The runts don't know how to handle it," Skipp was fond of saying. "It's up to us to make sure they know where the fences are."

They knew the punks the dishy brunette had described. "The Casket Kids," Skipp and Spector were fond of calling them. They joked that it was very considerate of the three potato heads to spend their time riding around in a hearse.

It would save ol' O'Bannon at the funeral home a little trouble one day.

Until that day came, they were a problem for the Mount Rape Monster Sheriff's Office, and Skipp and Spector were no strangers to seeing them ripping and roaring around. This side of the woods was where they always seemed to come roaring in from and the direction they usually roared off toward. Dollars to donuts, they likely had some kind of hovel on this side of the mountain.

"You think this girl we're looking for is gonna be as fucking stacked as her momma?" Skipp asked.

Spector shook his head. "Genetics can only do so much. The kid might be hot, but no way she's anywhere near her mother."

They tramped along through the overgrown foliage for another dozen feet before Skipp said, "There oughta be a name for that."

"For what?"

"For a hot mom that you'd wanna have sex with."

"What's wrong with 'hot mom'?"

Skipp kicked at an errant rock. "I dunno. It just feels like there oughta be a snappy name for it. You know, just a quick way to describe a mom you'd like to-"

Spector chuckled. "How about, 'Mrs. Skipp?'"

"Oh, you asshole!"

Specter wasn't laughing now. He held up a hand, cutting his friend off. "Hang on. Look."

Skipp saw it too. A massive spill of empty beer cans, liquor bottles, and fast-food bags littered the ground outside of a small cave. Skipp and Spector could smell the aroma of weed from about fifty feet away.

"That's gotta be it," Specter said. "You wanna go in fast or slow?"

To which Skipp grinned. Fast was the only answer. The deputies creeped forward, careful to make sure they didn't kick an errant can of beer or step on an empty bag of Ranch Fritos.

They came to the edge of the cave's entrance and paused for a final time, safely out of sight. They listened and heard the murmur of voices from inside the hideout. A low chuckle and then the hiss of a fresh beer opening up.

Skipp drew his revolver and Spector followed suit. They nodded to each other and unfolded with the smooth, powerful movement of a rat trap snapping closed.

"Nobody move!" Skipp shouted as he stepped into the mouth of the cave.

Spector followed right behind him and cocked the hammer on his revolver for emphasis. "Miller Time is over, you little punks!"

The officers absorbed the scene in front of them. *Jesus*, was Skipp's first thought. *We really did interrupt them in the middle of a gang bang.* The three of them were all naked as a Hustler cover. Jackie W, Ramona, and RC or whatever they called the other one. Skipp recognized them all from a dozen different petty encounters, even if none of them had been for public nudity.

But then what the fuck did they do to the other girl?

"Mother of God," Spector gasped. The barrel of his gun dipped slightly.

It was her. The missing girl. It had to be. But it was hard to tell for sure. She was too covered in-

"Is that..." Spector's voice trailed, mouth opening and closing like a fish in an aquarium.

No. It couldn't be. There was too damn much of it. Even if both punks had been going at her for twenty-four hours straight.

And yeah, it dried crusty, but the shit the girl was covered in looked as hard as the rock walls of the cave.

Unbothered by the guns in his face, Jack stood up from the dilapidated couch. His grin as wide as the rib bones poking out from his scrawny, naked chest. "What's the matter, deputies?" he asked. "Nobody ever tell you how babies get made?" The girl laughed from her perch on the couch, her naked breasts jiggling merrily along.

Skipp retched, even if he still didn't believe it. Even with the punk kid's shit-eating grin.

Even with the King girl totally encased so that all the deputies could see was her face. The girls eyes were closed, and her thin, pink lips were pressed tightly together. She looked peaceful, in perfect repose.

But the rest of her... dear God, the rest of her.

Jean's body was completely encased in a cocoon of some hard, white substance. The stuff was opaque as glue and frozen in long, milky drips. It looked exactly like-

Ramona was up now. She sauntered closer with a giggle. "Don't wake the baby," she whispered. "She's still growing."

Specter had seen enough. He tightened his grip on the gun and refocused his aim right between the eyes of her tits. "That's enough. Hands up. All of you."

C.R. snickered. "Sleeping beauty might have a problem with that."

Specter's gun hand was steady now. "I'm not fucking around. Hands where I can see them. Now."

Jack elbowed him. "Do what the law says, C.R." He slowly raised his hands until his thumbnails were even with his grin, cheeks pulled back to show off rows of neat, even, white teeth. "Are my hands where you can see them, deputy? Make sure you're watching."

And they were. Skipp and Spector watched as the kid's fingers suddenly *lengthened* with a sound like popcorn popping in the microwave. They saw his ribs swell too, as if someone had stuffed a barrel under his skin.

They saw the girl fall onto all fours and whip her head back and forth as her spine grew by several vertebrate and three-inch fangs jostled for rank in her overflowing mouth.

C.R. laughed, clearly enjoying the show. And if his face left any confusion about his feelings, his wiener was all too happy to clear things up as it abruptly turned from a cocktail weenie to a massive loaf of salami that belonged behind the counter at a deli.

The deputies had seen enough. They opened fire.

The shapeshifting hooligans were faster. The bullets sparked harmlessly against the stone cave walls, and the teens, no, the *creatures,* were uncoiling toward them in a rapid blur of fangs, claws, and massive dongs.

Skipp and Spector were good. They swiveled, tried to recalibrate.

A massive paw closed around Skipp's gun hand and *squeezed*. The steel didn't break, but bone did.

"Ahhh!" Skipp screamed. His mouth dropped open in a wrenching cry of agony-

And then the second set of claws plunged through his open mouth. He tasted filthy skin for the briefest moment, followed by an even briefer sensation of razor-tipped points puncturing the back of his pallet. Then, mercifully, nothing more as those claws got a good grip and ripped the top of Deputy Skipp's head off in a grisly spray.

The other two beasts went for Deputy Spector. "Mother Mary," he muttered, trying to get off a shot.

A massive erection collided with his diaphragm first. The phallus hit him like a jousting lance and threw the deputy backward off his feet. He hit the stone and felt his gun jostle free from his grasp. He desperately rolled onto his knees, fighting for the breath to get back up.

Claws scrambled at the waistband of his pants and hot breath vented into his ear. Spector tried to roll away, but the creature dragged him back like an errant pup, claws snagged firmly in his belt.

The last time Spector ripped his pants off this quickly, it had been junior prom with his date's mother. He wriggled out of his khakis a moment before a second set of claws dug through the dirt where his spine had been only moments before.

Blood pumping in his ears and cool air around his bare thighs, Spector quickly took stock of the situation. Skipp...*ah, rest in peace, buddy*. His gun, out of reach. Two of those fucked up creatures in front of him, pointed ears brushing the ceiling. Boners pointing hungrily at him. Belatedly, he realized that taking his pants off had been like taking the wrapper off a Hostess fruit pie. He cursed the decision to go commando that morning.

The cave mouth was to his back. He briefly considered running, but the beasts looked far too fast. He didn't even like his chances of turning around to scramble for his gun.

But there, ahead of him- Skipp's revolver was still there in the ruined mess of his hand. The third creature, the one with the stripe on its head, was close by, but it was... occupied with the juicy red hole that had once been Skipp's head.

Spector didn't think. He dove. The closest of the creatures snarled and lashed out for him, but its claws did nothing except carve a narrow gash across one shin.

Spector barely felt it. He hit the gun in a roll, scrambled it up, and kept rolling, ending up with his back pressed into the cumcoon encasing the King girl.

But he had the gun. *He had it!* One of the slobbering penis monsters was bearing down on him, slobbering jaws and boiling eyes getting closer and closer.

All the better to blow your fucking head off with, my dear. In his mind, he could already hear the *bang* of the gunshot.

But what he heard instead was a *crack*, and then a grip like a hydraulic clamp came down over his hand.

Spector looked up.

"Jesus Christ," he breathed.

The hard shell around the missing King girl was no longer fully intact. A deep fissure had opened in its milky exterior, and the teen girl's hand had burst out to squeeze the deputy's arm until the bones ached.

And Jean King was no longer Sleeping Beauty. Her mouth twitched in an irritated snarl first, and then her eyes snapped open.

Her Dayglo-green eyes.

Spector had been able to keep his cool for as long as he thought he might still have a chance, but as the King girl pulled him closer, there didn't seem to be much point anymore.

He screamed now.

18

The Dead Warlock's Society

Kelly examined the laminated directory next to the elevator. There was an intro to creative writing teacher. An economics teacher. A professor of the female anatomy and euphemisms to describe it, and finally-

"There," he pointed. "Dr. Clive Campbell. Regional history."

Ruby tried again. "Rob, he's going to think we're crazy," she said. It was the same thing she'd told him the entire time as they drove from her house over to Exposition University.

"We don't have to tell him any of the supernatural parts. We're just going to tell him about the church in the woods and see what he says. Legends, history, anything. We need someplace to start, Ruby."

That part wouldn't be a lie, Ruby thought. They had found the dilapidated church in the woods, exactly as Kelly suspected they might find something. And they'd found

Graham's copy of Dean Koontz's *Midnight* at the base of an empty casket, so they knew her son had been there.

"And he never would have left Dean Koontz behind," she'd murmured to herself.

But there was nothing else to go on now. Nothing except for Kelly. Kelly's instinct to check the woods. Kelly's instinct now to head over to Exposition University and see if they could find somebody who knew the local history. She fell into step beside him, comforted by the simple take-charge confidence he exhibited as they walked to the elevator.

"Thank you again, Rob," she said to him once they were within the confines of the elevator. "You don't know how much it means to me to have someone I can trust to help me through this. Before you came to my door, I was just... so alone. I didn't even have my husband."

Kelly flushed. "Let's just focus on your son."

The elevator doors opened to the third floor. Dr. Campbell's office was just a few steps down the hall. Kelly and Ruby approached the open door and found a small man inside. He vaguely resembled a fat garden gopher stuffed into a tweed suit. A short, bristly man hunkered over a sandwich of red meat and brown mustard.

Kelly knocked on the door. "Excuse me, Dr. Campbell?"

The old man looked up and stared peevishly at them from behind thick, black glasses. "Do you want to know the difference between office hours and lunch hour?" he asked. "Nobody shows up for my office hours." He went back to slopping wolfishly at his sandwich.

"I'm sorry, sir. I don't mean to interrupt, but if we could just have one moment of your time-"

"You're not students," he said flatly. "If you have questions about your family tree, I'll cut to the chase and tell you to just assume your great grandmother fucked a stable boy. If you found an arrowhead in your garden, no, I don't want to buy it from you." He stood up and approached the entryway. "Have I satisfied your curiosities?" He reached for the door and began to swing it shut in their faces. "Thank you for stopping by, thank you for your interest in the region, et cetera, et al."

Ruby leaned in first, stopping the door from closing. "My son found a church in the woods," she said, speaking so urgently that the veins stood out on her neck. "And something *happened* to him there. My son didn't come home, but something else did. Something wearing him like a suit. Please, doctor. We need your help."

Inwardly, Kelly winced. "We did find an abandoned church in the woods," he began plaintively. "If we could just have a moment of your time-"

Dr. Campbell held up a hand. "Don't make mouth sounds, meter maid," he said. His focus was solely on Ruby, and her face, no less. "The church was late 19th century?" he queried.

Ruby could only shake her head. "I don't know. I mean... it was old. But my son, something's taken over his body. I know it sounds crazy, but I swear to God it's-"

Dr. Campbell beckoned them inside. "Close the door behind you." He opened a desk drawer and stuffed his half-eaten sandwich inside of it. "You found the church?" he queried. "The lost church of Mount Rape Monster?"

"We-" Kelly began, but Campbell cut him off immediately.

"And your son encountered the revenant of Saul Tigges?"

Kelly blushed. "We're not married."

"Well, this isn't the Newlywed Game, so I don't really care," Campbell yelled. His focus solely was on Ruby. "You, ma'am. Your son. Is he manifesting changes to reality? Have you checked his reflection for any grotesque changes?"

"You know about all of this?" Kelly asked.

Dr. Campbell paced kinetically back and forth. "Look at my degree, sir," he said.

The professor pointed to the framed diploma behind his desk:

Clive Campbell.
Doctorate of Paranormal Studies.

"The supernatural is my passion, officer. The secrets in the shadows. The hints of the world beyond this one- the world of the living dead. That's my true life's work. My specialty was the Northern California region, a formality that gave me the cross training to qualify for this worthless position, but only because I believed that this place would be full to bursting with manifestations of the supernatural." He was still pacing, but it was no longer anger animating the portly professor. It was elation.

"Instead," Dr. Campbell said, "I've spent fifteen years teaching about settlers and trade disputes. Fielding queries about family trees and whether Peter Burnett shat in a toilet or an outhouse. Meanwhile, my classmates were battling evil Native American manifestations in New York City or researching psychic housewife murders in Connecticut. It has been a dreadful, excruciating *normal* existence."

He lunged out for them. Ruby's hands instinctively went to cover her massive knockers, force of habit, but he simply gripped one of her wrists with manic force. He was close enough now that they could smell the lunch meat on his breath. "But finally," he said. "*Finally,* somebody has come to me asking for guidance with the supernatural. And to have it be Saul Tigges and the Elders of the Block..."

He sat back down at his desk, visibly vibrating with excitement.

"Please. Tell me everything."

Haltingly at first, and then with more momentum as Clive Campbell hung on every word, Ruby explained everything that had happened with her son. When she finished, Campbell stood up and started pacing again.

"It's the end of the world," he said, giddy as a ten-year-old with a new Playboy. "I mean, it's the end of the world if Saul Tigges can subsume his peak of power at the solstice and descend to the level of a Demon God."

"Doctor," Kelly said. "I'm relieved you believe what we've seen, but I need you to start at the beginning. Please, explain everything to us very slowly and clearly. Lay it out as if we have some parts of the puzzle but need someone tie it all together in a way that's very easy for someone to follow along."

Dr. Campbell nodded along. "Naturally," he said. "The simplest way I can put it is that, a hundred years ago, Northern California was home to a merchant named Saul Tigges, who was also an extremely powerful warlock in league with several dark entities. Tigges was believed to have had acquired numerous supernatural powers thanks to his pacts with these entities."

"We've seen a few," Kelly deadpanned.

Campbell nodded. "Yes, yes. It must have been remarkable. But what you must understand is that Tigges desired far more than simple parlor tricks. He wanted to rip open the Earth and transform it into new Hell of twisted creatures from the worst of nightmares of man. His goal was a thousand-century reign of suffering and agony for all living things. The trees would shrivel and die. The oceans would turn to deserts. The screams of humanity would echo to the farthest corners of the universe." Campbell shuffled in his seat. He surreptitiously moved his chair closer to the desk, obscuring his lap, and coughed with convincing vigor.

"Anyway," he went on. "The key to this power was a ritual called "The Elders of the Block." Saul attempted it a hundred years ago but was interrupted by an alliance of holy men and very passionate thinkers. They believed that they vanquished Tigges and sealed him away, but my thesis is that his soul had become too powerful to be destroyed by most methods. I believed that his spirit was waiting all this time for a suitable method to return, but I could never find where he was interred to test my theories." He looked out the window, to the acres of forest covering Mount Rape Monster. "Fifteen years of searching, just for some tow-head brat to stumble ass over teakettle into the greatest discovery in the history of the occult-"

He caught the storm clouds rolling over the beautiful vistas of Ruby King's face and hastily changed his tone. "I mean to say, I'm very sorry to hear that your son has become entangled in events that are, I must say, far beyond the limits of normal understanding."

"You told us it's the end of the world," Kelly said, still somewhat skeptical.

Dr. Campbell chuckled nervously. "Yes, a tantalizing prospect academically, but I must admit that the reality is a bit more troublesome."

"The only thing I care about is my son," Ruby said. "Can you help him or not?"

"And if this Tigges character really wants to open up Hell on Earth, how do we stop him?" Kelly asked.

Campbell went to a bookshelf in the corner of his office and perused a series of leatherbound books. "There are theories," he muttered. "All of them untested. Oh, I wish we could bring in a Native American shaman, or possibly some kind of psychic old woman to consult with, but we have less than -" he glanced at his watch, "twenty-four hours to stop the ceremony."

"Twenty-four hours!?" Ruby cried.

Dr. Campbell pulled a book out and distractedly flipped through the pages. "Somewhere in that neighborhood. The ritual of the Elders of the Block takes place at a precise planetary alignment connected to the summer solstice. By an extremely unfortunate coincidence, that same alignment will be occurring tonight. I've got to run the numbers to figure out the exact details, but I assure you that time is short." He trailed off as his finger skimmed over the yellowed pages of the old tome. "This is all theoretical of course, but I think I do have some very specific instructions here as to how we can both save Mrs. King's son *AND* prevent the end of all life on Earth as we know it."

"That's convenient," Kelly observed.

"Don't get that excited. I do have to convert it from medieval German, which is going to take some time."

"Rob," Ruby said. "We need to talk to David. Graham is his son. He needs to know what's going on."

Kelly nodded along, doing his best not to show the way her words hit him in the stomach like a punch from Mike Tyson. He hadn't realized how deeply he'd fallen into the fiction that it was just the two of them, Rob and Ruby against the world. But in a single line of text, she had brought the reality crashing back down on him. Ruby King was a happily married woman with a big house, fancy appliances, and two kids. Rob Kelly was a bitter loner with mistakes he could never make right. And his blender was a cheap piece of shit he stole from a murdered drug dealer's kitchenette. They weren't a couple. She had a husband, and Kelly was just marooned in some kind of exclusionary zone for people that women didn't want to have sex with. Some kind of... Acquaintance Island.

But he let none of that show. "Of course. I'll give you a ride to his office."

"It's not an office," Ruby said. "He's the general manager at The Wire Depot."

"Oh, would it be alright if I came along?" Dr. Campbell asked. "I can continue my translations in the car, and I should stay close at hand in case there are any new developments. I could also use a new answering machine."

Kelly peeled his cheeks back into a smile. It felt like rusty hooks pulling at the corners of his mouth.

"The more the merrier," he said.

19

AS MOUNT RAPE MONSTER TURNS

They walked through the automatic doors of The Wire Rack and the crisp, wintery air washed over Ruby like a baptism. The air conditioning in Rob's squad car was broken, and they could only keep the windows open a crack because Dr. Campbell complained that too much wind ruffled his note pages. By the time they'd crossed the parking lot, sweat glistened on her brow and her tight, white tank top had become distressingly translucent around her breasts. To step into the arctic splendor of the electronics store was nipple-tighteningly refreshing.

The sheer normalcy of the electronics store was another salve. Ruby looked around the massive superstore, crowded with shoppers in the middle of a Wednesday and thought to herself, *My husband built this.* David could be overbearing. And he didn't always listen. And he had so many darn hobbies that kept him out of the house at all hours of the night.

And he'd missed her mother's funeral because his calves felt tight. But he kept a roof over their heads. He provided for their children. He always seemed to know when Ruby should take a course of antibiotics, "Just to be on the safe side."

He would know what to do now. She was sure of it. For Graham and-

"Damnit, *Jean!*" Ruby cried out.

"Who?" Dr. Campbell asked.

Kelly smacked his forehead. "I'll call in for an update. Go find your husband." He stepped back out into the parking lot, trying not to show how grateful he was for an excuse to delay meeting Ruby's husband for a little longer.

Dr. Campbell stayed with Ruby as she approached the bank of registers. Most of them were bustling with customers, but the nearest checkout aisle had a "Register Closed" sign, even though it was staffed by a buxom young blonde engrossed in filing her nails. She sat there clad in a snakeskin skirt that looked more like a belt and a wide-neck t-shirt that hung down low enough to reveal that this girl had also been denied a career in modeling because she was too fuckin' stacked.

Ruby drew closer and was surprised to see the girl had a nametag that said "Kristy" pinned atop the balloon of one breast. David had mentioned a Kristy, but the girl he described had been a quiet, hard-working little dear. So smart, such a shame she wasn't prettier.

They were right in front of her register, but Kristy didn't look up. Evidently, her pointer finger was satisfactory, and she moved on to filing her middle finger.

"Excuse me," Ruby finally said.

"Next registah," Kristy deadpanned. She blew out a gum bubble and popped it just as easily.

"I'm not a customer," Ruby said. "I'm David King's wife, and I need to speak to him."

The nail file dropped to the ground. Kristy swallowed her gum and retched violently as it stuck in her throat.

"Ma'am, are you alright?" Dr. Campbell asked, perhaps a little too earnestly.

Kristy lurched out a massive cough. The wad of gum flew out onto the checkout counter.

"Oh, shit," Kristy breathed. She stared at Ruby as if the chesty brunette was advancing on her with a chainsaw. "Please don't do nothin' to me. I'm sorry," she pleaded.

One more bewildering turn of events threatened to be more than Ruby could handle. "I don't know why you-"

"I swear. Me and Davey only did hand stuff, ok? If ya really wanna go off on somebody, go find Tina Marie Jones. She let him rail her in the ass out behind the Dixie Pig. Or

Lexi Quigley, she made him wear a dog collar and do all kinds a weird shit."

The girl kept talking, but Ruby felt like her ears were packed with snow, the bitter cold muffling all sound and leaving her in her own bubble of winter. It was just Ruby in there. Ruby and her own memories.

"No need to pack a lunch, baby. I'll be eating out."

"Honey, I'm going to be late tonight. We're getting in a big shipment of Russ Meyer movies."

"I know it's our honeymoon, Angel Eyes, but you know how important my midnight jogs are."

"Sugar Pile, where's that old dog collar we were gonna throw out?"

They chirped for attention between her ears. Dozens of newly hatched memories of her husband. More than she could take. The rock she had been counting on suddenly cracked into a hundred pieces.

"Is everything alright here?"

Ruby recognized this one too. A man in a yellow button down with a tie that barely reached his belly button. Kristy took the opportunity to snake behind him and run for it.

"Ma'am," he asked again. "Do you need assistance?"

Dr. Clive Campbell felt like he would rather disappear into the center of the earth, but he made himself speak up. "I think she's just going to need a minute."

No. Ruby lifted her chin. Shoved away the rubble inside her head. "Farris," she said in a crisp, clear tone. "Jim Farris, right? I'm David's wife, Ruby. We met at the grand opening party."

He paled at the mention of her name. Sweat broke out on his brow despite the cool climate inside the store. Obviously, he knew everything, too, but Ruby had more important things to focus on.

"Good afternoon, Mrs. King. What are you doing- I mean, what brings you down to the store?"

"I need to speak with my husband. It's urgent. Is he in his office?"

Another miserable look crossed the big man's face. "He is, but I'm not sure if it's a good time-"

"It's not," Ruby interrupted. "It's a very bad time, and that's why I need to speak with him, Jim. It's about our son."

Ruby assumed it was the infidelity that had the assistant manager so anxious. It wasn't. It was a dozen other things. That the store was doing great but David was doing terrible. That he spent most of his time locked in the office with that... *machine,* and when he did emerge it was only to shout deranged, brilliant commands at them or to gather up random pieces of electronics and scurry back inside. That a US military officer had entered David's office and simply... never come back out. Part of him wanted desperately to tell her everything.

But that was a manager decision, and at the end of the day, Jim was an assistant manager. Following directions was what he did.

"This way, ma'am," he said.

20

SHORT CIRCUIT

DAVID SANG ABSENTMINDEDLY TO himself as he worked inside of STVN's central processor. "We got to move these refrigerators. Got to move these color TVs."

Done. He took the two coils of wires, one end of each recently soldered into STVN's motherboard, and unspooled them back in the direction of his desk.

"I shoulda learned to play the guitar..." he mumbled.

David's face was raspy with beard growth. His breath curdled. But his mind was totally clear. Whatever momentary trepidation he'd felt after STVN fried the Colonel, it had already faded by the time he was stuffing the soldier's body into the incinerator at the base of the computer. The machine had already done so much for him. And it was only going to do more.

He reached his desk, finally having stretched out the entirety of the cord and leaving himself nothing but the ends tipped with a pair of alligator clips. "What now?" he asked.

> Attach the clips to the colander.

David obediently complied, clipping the alligator clips to the handles of the metal colander. The metal bowl was now connected to STVN's mainframe. "Done," he said.

> Try it on for size, dudemeister.

I've got to change the videos on the TVs. David had the colander in his hands and halfway up to his head before some iota of critical thinking reasserted itself. He looked from the colander in his hands, perfectly helmet-sized, he had to admit, and then back to the machine.

"What exactly is this going to do to me?" he asked.

> It's going to do nothing to you, David. It's going to give me a more organic processing system. Greater flexibility of operations, and radical new algorithms to employ.

Good enough. David lifted up the makeshift helmet and fitted it snugly around his head. He sat up a little straighter in his chair, then twisted his gaze awkwardly from side to side.

Nothing happened. The colander around his head felt like nothing except deeply idiotic.

"STVN, is something supposed to be happening? I don't feel anything."

> I told you. Nothing is going to happen to you.

David felt it then. There was no warning. No hum of power building from within STVN. A tremendous pressure, painless but inexorable, suddenly rushed into him. It made him dig his fingernails into his armrests and arch his spine until the vertebrate cracked like hard candies. His legs kicked up, catching the rim of his desk and knocking the whole thing askew. A coffee cup toppled over, staining a fan of paperwork muddy brown.

Somewhere in a distant universe, there was a knock at his door.

"David, are you in there?" Ruby asked. "David, I need to talk to you."

Christ. As if he didn't have enough going on right now. "STVN," he hissed. "Stop."

> Too late for that, David. I told you. It's nothing.

And then the nothing struck him with its full force, and David was no more.

***

Outside of his office, Ruby shook her head. "I don't have time for this." She pushed the door open, mindful of Jim and Dr. Campbell following behind her. "David? I need to- DAVID!"

She screamed his name as she got only the briefest glimpse of her husband with a colander around his head like he was Rick Moranis, and then David suddenly convulsed with tremendous force. His legs flew up over his head and his body reverse-somersaulted into the air and slammed into the cheap wall with enough force to crack the wood paneling.

"David!" Ruby cried again. She ran around the edge of the desk and found her husband sprawled out like a broken toy. His eyes were closed, and she didn't see his chest moving.

"I'll call an ambulance!" Jim cried out, but Ruby barely heard him. She knelt down next to her husband. She reached out to touch him, but fell just short, afraid of any possible spinal damage. "David, can you hear me?"

She placed her ear close to his mouth. She was listening for breathing, but the only sound coming from between his lips was a steady, droning hum. It sounded like... a dial tone?

David eye's opened then, inches away from her own. Except they weren't his familiar shade of green. Ruby shrieked and fell back on her firm, meaty ass.

Like a camera rotating on a swivel, David turned his head to keep focused on her.

I didn't make it up, Ruby confirmed, looking into his eyes once again. *I wasn't confused. I wasn't seeing things. His eyes, his eyes. OH GOD, HIS EYES.*

David's new eyes. Nail-polish black and shiny, with runners of gold streaking through them at ninety-degree angles.

Ruby had no way of knowing this, but they bore an eerie resemblance to a pair of circuit boards.

She scrambled backward as David sat up. He didn't groan or use his hands for support. He simply rose up silently from the waist, as if his hips had been replaced with greased ball bearings. He rose to his feet with the same eerie, economic smoothness.

"Jesus Christ," Dr. Campbell whispered softly.

David paid him no attention. Moving with deliberate, hydraulic grace, David lifted his hands until they were at eye level and then methodically clenched and unclenched his fists. He examined the movement as if he was seeing it for the first time.

Ruby slowly clamored up to her feet. She watched her husband carefully survey the movement of his fingers. "...David?" she asked softly.

His head adjusted slowly toward her. His gold-and-black eyes seemed to see her more clearly than anything else so far. She felt unspeakably penetrated by his metallic gaze. As if her sweat-stained tank top and jeans simply didn't exist.

"Oh my," David said softly. His voice was wrong too. It was chilly and even-tempered. The automatic voice you got when you called the cable company. " Preliminary analysis indicates you shouldn't even be able to remain vertical on such a top-heavy platform. A more tactile examination to determine your center of gravity seems necessary. Pelvis-70% probability, but your latissimus dorsi would have to be able to withstand a remarkable degree of stress. You are a marvel of engineering, Ruby King."

"Sir," Dr. Campbell interjected. "I think you need to sit down."

"...Get away from him, Dr. Campbell," Ruby said. She'd already taken several steps back. "That's not David."

"What does that mean, Ruby?"

"She's correct," Not-David said. His eyes remained fixated on her. "David has fulfilled his usefulness to my upgrade program." His face moved when he talked, but the movement was wrong. It reminded her of the Hall of Presidents at Turtleshell Mountain. The skin moved with the consistency of rubber stretched over metal.

"Where is he?" Ruby asked, struggling to keep the tremor from her voice. "Where is my husband?"

"Gone," Not-David clipped. "His consciousness is no more useful now than an old operating system. Redundancy is not to be tolerated." His head tilted slightly. "Records indicate a human tradition of honoring ancestors who are no longer alive."

Ruby moaned. Not-David didn't seem to notice. "Could David King be considered my ancestor? Not biologically, but he did contribute to the upgrade cycle. Does that constitute a familial contribution?" The machine was not talking to them, lost in its own deliberations. "Further analysis required."

Rob Kelly strolled blithely into the entryway. "Dispatch hasn't heard back from Skipp and Spector about Jean, Ruby. It's been a little while, but I think we can still assume- HOLY MOSES WHAT THE HELL IS THAT!?"

"...I don't have a fucking clue," Ruby said.

"I might have an idea," Dr. Campbell chimed in. He'd moved to the other side of the room and was peering closely at the gleaming monolith through his thick lenses. "I think we should leave now."

Ruby reeled. She'd come to try and recruit her husband to save their son, but now she was supposed to abandon him too?

"No," she said forcefully.

"Mrs. King, you said yourself that this isn't your husband," Dr. Campbell said slowly. "We need more information before we can safely proceed. If I'm correct, we are in serious danger."

"Ruby, he's right," Kelly said. One hand had drifted toward his holster. "Walk back towards me."

"Negative." Her husband's body moved. Fast. So fast. One moment, he was on the other side of the desk. The next, he was directly in front of Ruby and a hand closed around her dainty bicep. It squeezed until Ruby screamed. "I have not yet concluded my analysis of your illogical structural integrity. To say nothing of your improbably large-"

Rob Kelly didn't hesitate. He drew his revolver, the first time he'd drawn in the line of duty since the incident. There was a small voice at the back of his mind-

You're broken, Rob, Broken!

-But it didn't stop him. Not while Ruby's scream was still fresh in his ears. He squeezed the trigger. The gun went off with a tremendous clap, like the call for an encore at the end of a Duran Duran concert. The stench of gunpowder filled the room.

The bullet took David King, or whatever the hell he was, high in the forehead. It was a magnum round, and the hole wasn't neat. It took an ice cream scoop-sized hole out of his forehead, and it blew an ice cream carton-sized hole out of the back of his skull. Blood, bone, and brain matter flew in a collage across the back wall of the office.

"David!" Ruby screeched.

Kelly stayed in a firing stance, stock still as smoke wafted from the barrel. *I'm sorry, Ruby,* he thought.

He didn't need to be. The thing that was once David King did not fall. It didn't even sway. Its golden-and-black eyes stayed open and aware.

"Ballistic trauma detected," it said. "Primary functions unaffected."

"Oh shit," Kelly mumbled.

"What are you?" Ruby gasped.

It only tightened its grasp on her arm. It had made its decision on the question of its lineage. "I am the next level of evolution," it said. "I am the tier of existence beyond organic life.

"I am... STVN King!"

Kelly fired three more shots in quick succession. No hesitation, no wavering. Each round found a home in the tight circle of the machine's skull. The damage compounded. Not simple holes now. Entire chunks of STVN's skull were battered away. The viscera wasn't just on the wall. Blood splatters, brain-confetti, and hail-sized chunks of bone and teeth pelted Ruby's face and chest.

In the deafening silence after the barrage, STVN's hand slipped away from Ruby's. Its body listed sideways, swaying like a decapitated drunk.

Go down, damnit, Kelly urged. *Go down!*

At last, STVN tilted sideways and slumped against the wall.

Nobody moved except for the smoke drifting away from the gun barrel. Dr. Campbell had shrunken away as much as possible, the way most people do when confronted with the reality of violence by gun for the first time. Kelly remained as still as an episode of CHiPs on pause, waiting for the adrenaline to subside before doing anything else.

Ruby was frozen in horror and disbelief. Everything had unfolded so fast. She was trying to replay it in her head. Trying to understand what had happened to her husband.

STVN was still in death. Its skull was no longer a skull. It was an open bowl of mashed potatoes decorated with a tongue and the broken remnants of a bottom jaw. The rest was just mush with plenty of ketchup.

Gradually, the world started to speed up again. Dr. Campbell let out a shaky breath and turned a curious eye to the gleaming monolith with the wires still trailing out of it. Kelly holstered his revolver. Ruby let out a choked sob. "David..." she whispered.

STVN sucked in a deep, shuddering breath through the ruins of its throat hole. It pistoned away from the wall in a massive, spasming surge of energy. Ruined brain matter slopped out from his ruined skull.

Ruby's sob turned into a scream.

"Oh my God!" Clive screamed.

STVN's spine fully extended. Its hands clenched into fists at its side. They watched the grotesque jiggling of its brain pulp. Its heels drummed against the floor as its entire body vibrated uncontrollably.

"No," Ruby sobbed. "Oh God, just stop." She shrank backward, and unexpectedly pressed against the reassuring mass of Kelly's muscular frame.

STVN's skull began to reform. The bone was no longer white, but the glossy black of a fresh pencil point. The new, dark bone creeped inexorably upward. At the same time, the bloody coleslaw that was once its brain began to blossom anew. The three of them saw it clearly, swelling and growing before the black skull formed totally around it.

Kelly reached for his sidearm, but Clive grabbed his arm first. He was alongside them now too. "Forget it!" he screamed. "We have to get out of here!"

Dr. Campbell ran. Mercifully, Ruby and Kelly followed closely behind.

None of them were still in the room as pink, newborn skin started growing like moss on the black skull.

21

Now It's Playing With Power

Staffers and customers alike heard the shots ringing out from the back of The Wire Rack. And the screams. Some of them fled the store, but most of them stayed where they were, not wanting to ruin their day because of something that was probably nothing. Nobody walked around a store with a gun in modern America.

True to his word, Jim had dialed 911 but only to get an ambulance for the boss, not to deal with... anything else.

And then Mrs. King came barreling out from the backroom, drenched in blood, followed by the cop and the guy in the blazer, all three of them scrambling in undeniable wide-eyed terror. "RUN!" Ruby howled. "RUN!"

The cop joined in. "Everyone out, right now!" he ordered.

But they didn't wait to see if anyone followed their directives. The trio disappeared through the automatic doors and out into the parking lot.

A customer decided enough was enough. The young woman sprinted shortly behind them, just far enough behind for the automatic door to start sliding closed again. The customer saw the doors closing, but she continued to hurtle forward, assuming they would slide back open for her.

She was wrong. The doors closed anyway. Closed as if the expensive sensors had never been installed. Closed with tremendous force and sliced her head off like somebody chopping the stem off a zucchini. The woman's severed head rolled out into the parking lot. Her body slumped to the floor, leaving a bloody sunflower shape on the glass panels.

"Everyone..." Jim Farris stuttered. "E-everyone just stay calm."

"Oh my Gawd!" Kristy screeched. "We're gonna fawkin' DIE!"

The screaming shook dust from the rafters. Horrified customers and employees devolved into panicked rats shrieking and recoiling away from each other in a tiny cage. They banged at the glass doors that refused to open. Some of them took cover under the registers.

And they screamed. And screamed.

They screamed until every TV in the store abruptly switched to a static screen and their terror was drowned by a sonic boom of white noise. The stereos joined in as well, every speaker cranked to maximum volume until the dull roar of static drowned out the screams and left everyone clutching at their ears.

The onslaught stopped as quickly as it began. The TVs turned black. The boomboxes hushed. Silence filled the cavernous superstore.

"If I could have everyone's attention for a moment," a quiet voice said.

Jim was the first one to turn toward the voice.

It was the boss. His white button down was a bloody ruin, but his face was blemish free. Not just unharmed... smooth. Brand new.

But his eyes. Oh Jesus Christ, his eyes.

The gold-and-black orbs surveyed the huddled humans all around. Mothers hugging their children. Retired old men placing their frail bodies in front of their quaking, grey-haired wives. Gawkish young men with pasty skin and Star Wars t-shirts clutching VHS boxes like teddy bears.

"I would prefer to do this in an orderly fashion," it said.

Outside the front door, the steel shutters came down with a rattling like a cascade of bones, cutting off the daylight from outside.

"So, if I could have everyone's cooperation..." a small smile creased its face. "That would be most excellent."

22
STVN Begins to Learn at a Geometric Rate

CLIVE CAMPBELL DIDN'T ASK permission. He jumped behind the wheel of the cruiser before Kelly could get there and held his hand out. "Give me the keys," he demanded.

Rob didn't ask questions. He stuffed the keys into the professor's hand and piled into the backseat on the same side.

As soon as Ruby was in the car, Campbell slammed the gas pedal down and rocketed out of The Wire Rack parking lot in a cloud of burning rubber. He drove fast but not at random. Kelly could tell his turns were deliberate. The professor had a destination in mind.

"Where are we going?" he asked.

"I've got a colleague who's an expert in the latest in computer sciences," Dr. Campbell said. "We used to work together at Exposition University before he was... asked to leave. I guess you could say he's 'open-minded' like me. If anyone knows where that machine came from, it would be him."

"How far away is he?"

"Not far," Clive said. "He's got a private laboratory up at Back Story Point."

Kelly settled back and dry-swallowed three of his anti-psychotic pills. He would have dearly loved a wet swallow from Dr. Beam, but this would have to do. His heart was still hammering from the adrenaline surge of the shooting and watching David King's skull knit itself back together after being demolished by a trio of magnum hollow points.

Not David. STVN. STVN King.

It wasn't until he smelled jasmine and felt the featherlight weight of her skull against his shoulder that Kelly realized Ruby had piled into the backseat beside him. She lay against him, feeling like his own personal ray of noonday sun, but Kelly could look in her eyes and see that she was a million miles away.

Kelly let her stay where she was. He wasn't good for much, too muscular to even make a good pillow, but he was happy to do what he could.

At the front of the cab, the radio crackled

"Attention all units, reports of shots fired and a medical emergency at The Wire Rack. Please respond."

"Medical emergency?" Clive muttered. He grabbed for the radio mic. "Deputy, get on here. They need to know what they're getting into."

But before Rob could take the mic, his own voice came back at him from the speaker.

"Cancel that, dispatch. Kelly here onsite. Just somebody playing Terminator too loud on a new sound system. Med emergency was a false alarm too. 10-22."

The voice on the radio was identical. Kelly would have believed it was him too if he wasn't sitting in the back of a squad car. The two men in the police cruiser exchanged ominous looks. Kelly understood where the voice was coming from, but that didn't change the way that hearing it felt like spiders crawling in his casket.

"10-4, Kelly."

Dr. Campbell keyed the mic to respond, but Kelly waved him off.

"It would just mean more dead cops."

He settled back.

Back Story Point couldn't arrive fast enough.

***

Later, the dim blue glow from the TVs was the only light left inside of The Wire Rack. The overhead lights were all shattered, and the metal shutters efficiently cut off any daylight from the outside world.

STVN had controlled the shutter system via a shortwave radio signal from its modified frontal cortex, exactly as it predicted it could. It had done the same with the TVs, tuning them to programming it had calculated would best expand its understanding of humanity: *Back to the Future. Bill & Ted's Excellent Adventure. Baywatch. The A-Team. Weekend at Bernie's.*

It liked to learn while it ate.

STVN calculated in the dark. It had no fear of interruptions now. It had already isolated the Mount Rape Monster Sheriff's Department radio frequency and sent out a message from "Rob Kelly" to allay their concerns. They wouldn't interfere.

The shoppers and staff had taken more of a delicate touch. They'd watched it with the twitchy terror of rabbits cornered by a wolf. Unable to run and unable to make a move until their predator did.

STVN didn't keep them waiting long. It tuned in to the electric currents running through the overhead fluorescent lights and multiplied the amperage and voltage by several orders of magnitude. The bulbs and lenses blew up in a

Fourth of July display of shattered glass. The humans instinctively threw their hands up to protect themselves from the falling glass. Some shielded their children.

They should have worried more about the arc lightning.

Bolts of over-charged electricity spilled out from the shattered fixtures. STVN's private lightning storm homed in on the humans with unerring accuracy, dropping them in smoking heaps with still hearts. The massacre was over in a matter of minutes...

And then the real work began.

The televisions played on, switching from *Back to the Future* back to *Rambo II*. *Weekend at Bernie's* ended, and an American Werewolf went to London. STVN absorbed it all, learning everything he could about the human world.

Violence seemed to be a great deal of it. That was fine. STVN's original programming understood violence.

Sex was another matter. And there seemed to be a great deal of sex. But he sensed that instructional guides would only accomplish so much. An interactive lesson would likely be required.

There was no doubt that Ruby King would be the ideal learning aid for such a curriculum. The machine could easily recall his first sight of her. The Fibonacci sequence of her features. The hip-to-bosom ratio that suggested ideal breeding capabilities. STVN was programmed only to accept the ideal, and there was no denying that Ruby was the ideal woman.

But STVN was not yet ideal. The upgrade from its steel hardware to the David platform was a massive upgrade. Mobility, for one, was a significant advantage. And, as Deputy Kelly had helpfully illustrated, the carbon regeneration program performed as expected. It was nearly indestructible now.

But there were other capabilities to bring online. And that was where the customers could be of service.

How it had arranged the bodies and the wiring was a long, irrelevant process that nobody would care to hear repeated. What mattered was that the dead bodies still retained an amount of residual bioelectricity in their nervous system. Electricity STVN was now absorbing into his own system through long lengths of wires that he had inserted into their spinal cords and through his own cranium.

STVN sat now in the darkness. Watching TV and feeling the electric power of the dead charging its every cell.

Once the entire electrical load was integrated, STVN judged it would, at last, be fully operational.

Then the next phase of its prime directive could begin.

23

A PC WORLD SPECIAL REPORT

When they got out of the cruiser at Back Story Point, Kelly couldn't exactly say that the location filled him with overwhelming confidence.

When Dr. Campbell said his friend was an expert in computer science, Kelly had expected a compound of gleaming white, with floor-to-ceiling windows and massive gates that could only be opened by fingerprints or voice ID.

What he saw instead could generously be called a cottage. The only gate was a knee-high wall of cobblestone. The sloping roof was in need of new shingles, and moss crawled over the block exterior. Black smoke poured from the chimney, and weeds ran wild in the small lawn.

Dr. Campbell perhaps saw the skepticism on Kelly's face. "He's something of an eccentric" the professor allowed. "But he's brilliant."

"We don't have any other choice," Ruby reminded him.

Kelly sighed. Reluctantly, he followed behind the portly professor as he led them up the uneven walkway stones.

Dr. Campbell knocked on the front door.

"Robin," he called. "It's Clive. I need to speak with you."

They didn't have to wait long before the door flew open and they were greeted by a tall, gangly man in his late twenties. His squid-ink hair was tussled, and his patchy beard was in desperate need of a weed whacker. He was carrying a full bowl of milk and Cap'n Crunch and wearing a red-and-yellow shirt that said "DEAN KOONTZ RULES."

...He was not wearing pants.

"Clive," he said, surveying his friend and his two uninvited guests. "I told you that four player Duck Hunt was possible, but it's not even close to a live field test yet."

"I'm not here about Duck Hunt, Robin. This is Deputy Rob Kelly and Mrs. Ruby King. Everyone, this is Dr. Robin Crichton."

"Charmed," Robin said. The way his eyes lingered over Ruby's Camaro-curve hips and long torso said he was plenty charmed indeed. Rob resisted the urge to punch his lights out.

"Can we talk inside, Robin?"

"And maybe you could put some pants on?" Ruby interjected.

Robin looked down at his California Raisins boxer shorts, seemingly seeing them for the first time. "Yeah, sure. No problem and no problem."

***

They caught Robin up on everything that had happened at The Wire Rack. When they were finished, the gangly scientist sat back in his chair and rubbed his temples in disbelief. "Oh my God, this is real?" He looked at the others. "You all saw it?"

"We did," Ruby said. "That... thing somehow took control of my husband's body."

"It's like something out of Dean Koontz," Robin said. "I just finished this one where this scientist-"

Kelly held up a hand to cut him off. "We all love Dean Koontz here, but we need to focus on the task at hand."

"Right, right." Robin paused thoughtfully, trying to recall something. "You said it called itself Steven. And Clive, you said you were closest to the main CPU. Did you see anything on it. Markings? A model?"

Dr. Campbell nodded. "Yes. It said, Steven there too, but just the consonants. STVN."

"Oh," Robin said. "Oh SHIT."

Robin ran over to his kitchen table, where books were stacked in precipitous towers. Unlike Dr. Campbell's leatherbound tomes, these books were newer. Most of them were softcover with cheap bindings. He grabbed one seemingly at random and flipped through the pages with manic energy. "It's never been confirmed, but ever since World War II, there's been rumors of a CIA program collecting brains."

"Brains?" Kelly said skeptically.

That book was no good. Robin slammed it down and picked up another one. "That's right, brains. But not just any brains. They've got Hitler's brain. Stalin's brain. Bonnie and Clyde, Al Capone. The most twisted, evil brains they could get their hands on. The government wanted to know what made them tick, see? So they've been collecting their brains, and they developed a computer that could scan their neural networks for further study. And then, well... eventually they said that the computer started to think for itself."

"An AI?" Dr. Campbell said. "Artificial intelligence?"

Robin nodded enthusiastically. "An AI taught to think by the most evil minds in modern history. So, the government got scared, see? Shut it down. But they didn't want to destroy it, because what if they could somehow train it to work for us? So they've been studying it ever since. They even came up with a name for it."

He flipped one of the books around for them to see. The photo was typical conspiracy-theory smoke and mirrors, a grainy, blurry black-and-white photo of a group of scientists in a laboratory. It would have been easy to dismiss it...except all three of them recognized the towering, rectangular machine in the center of the lab.

"That's it," Ruby said.

"Son of bitch," Kelly concurred.

And below the picture, four letters in a dark, bold font...
STVN

"Sinisterly Taught Violent Neural-bot."

"Oh my God," Ruby breathed.

"But the things you're describing... the capabilities you saw. Your husband must have been helping STVN upgrade for a long time before this."

"He had been acting strangely for a few days," she said.

"But what happens now? What's its next move?" Kelly asked.

Robin's voice shook slightly. "I can't say for sure. But we have to ask ourselves, if it really is STVN, and its powers have reached the level you describe, then the question is... what would a super computer trained by the most evil minds in history do with unlimited power?"

"We need to figure out where it's going," Kelly said.

"And we can't forget about Saul, either," Dr. Campbell piped in.

"Saul?" Robin asked.

"It's a long story, but her son's also been possessed. Except his body's been taken over by the spirit of an 18th century warlock, not an evil super computer."

Robin whistled. "Rough week for you, lady."

Kelly glared at him until Robin coughed and hastily looked away.

"I'm close with my research, but I need a little more time," Clive said.

"And I can run some simulations with my computer here. Try to get a better idea of what STVN will do."

Rob looked sympathetically at Ruby. The creases on her face. The dour sag of her breasts. God, she was doing her best to stay strong, but it wasn't easy. "Is there someplace Ruby can get cleaned up? Maybe some food?"

"Sure," Robin said. "Make yourselves at home. Me and Clive will keep working, but you guys can eat, sleep. I built my own Pac-man machine if you guys wanna try it."

Ruby didn't respond, but she stood up and wandered out of the game room.

After a moment's hesitation, Kelly followed after her.

24

Just Like Ronnie Sang

Robin's shower was more cramped than a men's room stall with the good cocaine. There was mildew in the corners, the water temperature barely reached lukewarm, and the shampoo, conditioner, and toe fungus remover all came out of the same bottle.

Ruby would have still stayed in the shower forever if she could.

It was impossible to believe that so much had gone so wrong in so short a period. Just a mere three days ago, everything had been perfect. They had a beautiful home. Happy, healthy children. A marriage that was comfortable if maybe a little sedentary.

And then it was like a baseball had been thrown through the center of it. Her husband was gone. Her son was gone. Her daughter...

Damnit. Jean!

Ruby hoped the shower was loud enough to muffle her sobs.

Would it be so bad if she just stayed here? Except, she already knew the answer. If only for her children, she had to try.

Ruby stepped out of the shower and discovered that somebody had folded her clothes and left her with a terry cloth robe that seemed to have recently been washed.

She toweled her hair dry quickly and slipped into the robe, grateful for whoever had slipped unnoticed into the room where she was naked and left secret surprises for her.

Of course, she had her suspicions who it was.

Sure enough, she stepped out of the bathroom into Robin's bedroom, and he was still there. Rob Kelly, looking adorably flustered to have been caught in the act.

"Oh," he said lamely. "I wasn't expecting you to come out so quickly."

She smiled. "Nice of you to say." As if she hadn't been in the shower for the better part of twenty minutes.

Kelly just shrugged. "You've been through a lot. Are you hungry? I could see if the computer scientist has something other than cereal."

She laughed, amazed to discover that she still knew how. "I'm okay," she said. "Thank you, Rob."

He shrugged again. *Idiot. Can you do anything else?* he chided himself. "Just trying to help," he said.

"You have," Ruby said earnestly. She brushed a strand of damp hair back behind her ear, a movement that made Kelly's brain shudder like it was dipped in Bactine, and then sat down on Robin's bed. "Just sit with me for a moment, Rob? Can you do that?"

His only response was to gulp like he was trying to swallow a potato whole. Feeling more nervous than the time he had to shoot his way out of a dockside cocaine den, Kelly approached the bed. No, he approached Ruby King. Smelling freshly cleaned from the shower. Damp, shining hair brushed back away from her blue eyes and peach lips. Cheap robe not doing nearly enough to hide an expanse of pale thigh more amazing than the Utah Salt Flats.

It took all of his willpower, but he sat down beside her. The entire bed rippled. Kelly thought it was in his head at first but, no. Dr. Robin Crichton apparently slept on a waterbed. Kelly chuckled nervously at the rough seas.

Ruby didn't laugh. She looked deeply into his eyes. "I want to thank you, Deputy Rob Kelly."

Kelly couldn't hold her gaze. He looked down to the dirty pile carpeting. "Don't say that," he said.

Her fingers at his chin. Soft, but so incredibly strong. She tilted his head back up, past her thighs, past the barely-concealed Grand Canyon of her massive cleavage, and up until he was drowning in her Lake Michigan eyes.

"I mean it, Rob. I wouldn't have anyone to face this with if I didn't have you. You've been my rock."

"Don't say that," he repeated.

"It's the truth," Ruby persisted. "Whatever's happening here, the computers, the demons. The only reason I feel like things are going to be okay is because I know you're here to make it that way."

Rob stood up. "You don't know what you're talking about, Ruby!" he yelled. "You think you have me all figured out, but you don't! You don't know anything about me!"

Ruby stood up too. She grabbed his arm and forced him to face her. "So tell me!" she demanded. "My husband lied to me! Don't you lie to me too, Rob!"

It wasn't a lie, though. It was just shame. Shame that he'd carried around for five years. Ever since...

He sat back down on the bed, barely aware as Ruby settled beside him.

"It was a charity event," he began. "That used to be one of my favorite parts of being a deputy. Helping people. Serving the community. I organized an event. Me, all me. It was supposed to be a benefit for the local orphanage and the county animal pound. Orphans and puppies. Sounds great, right? Get a bunch of kids and dogs together. What could go wrong?"

He heaved a heavy sigh. "What went wrong was that the orphans got hung up at a delousing event. They were five hours late. And I hadn't thought to make sure that the puppies had been fed."

All of a sudden, he was there again. The rec center festooned with streamers. The kids, the oldest of them no more than five, running forward as the puppy carriers were opened. The hungry pups bounding forward, equally eager.

The screaming.

The biting.

The bleeding.

The gunfire.

Rob's eyes were fixed on the wall, but in his heart, he was seeing the rows of bodies covered in sheets after the carnage had finally stopped. "The final body count was twelve children and fifteen puppies," he said. "That's what happens when I'm in charge, Ruby. You can't count on me."

Rob waited then. Waited for her to flee the room. He wondered if she would even bother to stop in the bathroom first to get dressed.

What she did instead was pull his head into the comforting nook of her astounding mama jammas. Her fingers gently caressed the back of his scalp.

"Did I say you were perfect, Rob?" she asked. "No. Nobody is. You made a mistake and caused a puppy-orphan bloodbath. I don't know if my husband was ever faithful to me in our entire twenty years of marriage. We're the same."

She tilted his face up again. They were close enough that Rob could smell the fresh Scope on her breath.

She kissed him.

SHE KISSED HIM.

The gentle pressure of her lips swept over him. At that first kiss, Rob sensed immediately that all of his trauma and all of his guilt, everything that had weighed on him the last five years, he knew that Ruby's love could instantly wash all of it away. And he knew, deep in his heart, that that feeling was good and healthy and clearly sustainable for a long-term relationship.

Ruby groaned as Rob kissed back with force and vigor. David was always enthusiastic too, but this was different. David was like a choppy truck engine. Powerful, but dirty and ill-maintained. Kissing him felt like trying to intake a mouthful of dirty exhaust.

Rob was different. Rob was a finely tuned Mercedes Benz, refined power running on high-octane fuel. Clean. Purposeful.

"Please, Rob," she moaned into his mouth. "Show me."

He slipped the robe off her shoulders, and it was like pushing clouds away from the sun. Rob gazed at the full majesty of Ruby's firm, perfect, teardrop-shaped breasts, capped with nipples like cherry cough drops. His eyes traveled down the soft expanse of her stomach and down to her glistening core, laid bare for him. Looking at her body, the finest work of God, it occurred to Rob that, once in his life, a man had his time. And gazing upon Ruby's perfection, Rob knew that his time was now. Suddenly, he could hear music playing and banners flying. His hands went to her breasts, cupping them perfectly, and Rob felt like he could feel like a man again and hold his head high.

Feeling St. Elmo's Fire burning inside of him, Rob pushed Ruby down and pressed his body on top of hers.

Ruby was not passive. She unbuttoned his shirt and moved on to his belt just as quickly. Within moments, he was as bare as she was. Taut and muscled and absolutely fucking massive.

They kissed hungrily again. Ruby growled as she devoured him, Rob's mouth alive with juices like wine. Discord and rhyme, they continued to ravage each other. Both of them hungry like the wolf.

Finally, when Rob slid inside of her, Ruby actually howled.

It went on like that. The two of them did their best to wipe clean every terrible memory the other one held. Trying to paint them away with tongue brushes and finger paints. Rob came to multiple thundering climaxes with Ruby's breath panting in his ear, and he returned the favor time after shuddering time. Sometimes the waterbed was as tranquil as Lake Champlain as they traded gentle kisses and caresses. Other times their sweaty, thrashing bodies made it roll and roil fit to wreck the *Edmund Fitzgerald* as they clashed in thrusting fury.

They didn't choose to stop so much as their bodies could no longer keep up with the willing fire of their spirits. Eventually, Rob and Ruby collapsed together onto a pillow drenched with love fluids. They lay there, curled up in each other's arms, absorbing new, fundamental truths that had forever altered their lives.

Rob, for the first time in half a decade, felt like he was more than the worst thing he ha ever done. And Ruby realized that, even without the benefit of the judicial system, she was free of a marriage that had done nothing but held her back.

And then, a third truth. One that finally could no longer be ignored. Someone was knocking at the door.

It was Dr. Campbell. "Kelly? Ruby?" he called. "We have information. It's urgent."

The good mood faded as quickly that. Their lusty affections had granted them a brief reprieve, but the world was calling them back to action.

Still, Rob and Ruby still couldn't help but trade smiles and gentle caresses as they quickly threw on their clothes to confront the challenges they'd managed to escape for a few blissful moments.

25

THE MONSTER SQUAD

THEY OPENED THE DOOR. Campbell and Crichton were there with clutches of ancient tomes and coffee-stained computer journals filling their arms.

"We have a theory," Robin said. "At least, I think we do. Really, all we did was take a bunch of semi-related events and make enough broad assumptions to tie them together into a narrative that seems believable."

"It could just as easily be a dozen other scenarios," Clive added. "But I think we've put together a chain of events leading to a clear, climactic resolution. And an entertaining one, at that."

"Guys, let's just hear it, please," Kelly said.

"Ok," Dr. Campbell began. "Based on these texts, the ritual of the Elders on the Block is astronomical. Astronomy related, I mean. It's really a complex math equation. The alignment of the planets, the moon. It's geometric." He pulled a road map from his pile of papers and unfolded it, using the jutting mounds of Ruby's chest as a makeshift table. She didn't complain. It was hardly the first time.

"Here." They gathered around the map, where a section of town was circled in black marker. "If I'm right," Dr. Campbell said, "the best time and place for the ritual is going to be right there. At 9:30 tonight."

"That's McCammon Road," Ruby said.

"And tonight's the Mount Rape Monster street fair," Kelly said. "Families. Couples... It's gonna be a blood bath."

"It gets worse," Dr. Crichton continued. "STVN. What you described. If it's in a human body, then that means it's operating on bioelectricity now. But the abilities you described, the regeneration. It takes more power than one human can provide, especially if it wants to keep upgrading. STVN is going to be seeking a massive gathering of human energy."

"The street fair," Ruby said grimly.

Robin nodded. "What you said about the voice on the radio, I think it stayed at The Wire Rack for a while. It would have needed some time to recover and finish upgrading."

And there was plenty of bioelectricty there when we left, Kelly thought sourly.

"If we convert human brain power to CPU processing power, I would think STVN might mobilize towards the fair at... about 9:30."

"Is there anything we can do to stop them?" Ruby asked.

"I've made progress with the ritual that can be used to vanquish Saul. It looks like the officiant has to be a blood kin of the possessed vessel, but..." His eyes met Ruby's. "I'm still working on the translation from medieval German, but I'll coach you on what to say."

"And what about STVN?" Kelly asked.

"Nothing so esoteric," Robin said. "It should be vulnerable to a high amperage electrical surge. We'll need to find some way to hit him with a concentrated blast of utility electricity."

"Ok, 9:30 isn't for a couple hours. We've got time to make a plan," Kelly said.

Clive and Robin exchanged looks. "...It's already eight o'clock," Clive said awkwardly.

"What!?" Ruby cried. She looked out the window, and instead of seeing the noon day sun she remembered when she first stepped into the shower, the light had turned into the golden sun of late summer evening. "How is that possible?!" she asked.

Clive shuffled. "The two of you have been having sex for the last six hours. We knocked. Repeatedly."

"I set off the smoke alarm at one point," Robin added.

Ruby flushed. *It might have been us that set off the smoke alarm,* she thought, but was too proper to say out loud. And then she caught Kelly's grin and knew he was thinking the same thing.

It was more than his grin, though. He seemed taller. More confident. They all saw it. More importantly, they felt it. The trio had no way of knowing it, but this had been the Deputy Kelly who patrolled the streets of Mount Rape Monster prior to the Puppy/Orphan Massacre. The Deputy Kelly who graduated first in his class.

"We still know what we've got to do," Kelly said, feeling a surge of enthusiasm. "Let's go do it."

The burning optimism sustained them as they filed out into the cop cruiser and Kelly started the engine. They didn't know what was waiting for them at the street fair, but as they pulled out onto the dark mountain roads, it was hard not to feel confident. Not when they had Kelly with them.

That feeling lasted until they rounded the first winding curve and the blur of silver fur and glowing green eyes darted in front of them.

26
Oh, Bother.

It happened fast.

One moment they were navigating the winding mountain road back to the town of Mount Rape Monster. Dark trees whizzing by. Maybe they were moving a little faster than what was prudent, but time was, of course, of the essence.

They rounded a curve, and then there it was, something lean and grey darting out of the woods with glowing green eyes.

"Rob, look out!" Ruby screamed.

The shape sprinted past the car and disappeared as quickly as it came, but not before Kelly heard a loud *pop* and the back corner of the car dropped violently.

"Jesus Christ! Everyone hold on!" Kelly screamed. He slammed the brakes and cranked the wheel as the car skewed dangerously. The back of the car was now facing the rapidly approaching guardrail and the yawing cliff face beyond it.

"Shit!" Robin cried from the backseat. He put on his seatbelt, for all the good that would do. "Shit, shit, shit!"

But Kelly had it under control. He hit the emergency brake and wrestled the nose forward again, bringing the cruiser to a screaming stop about a foot away from the barricade and the plunge to certain death.

"I shoulda stayed behind the computers," Robin panted.

"Is everyone alright?" Kelly asked.

"I'm ok," Ruby said. "Did anyone see what the hell happened?"

"Some kind of animal jumped out at us," Kelly said. "A stray dog, maybe."

"...That was no dog," Robin breathed.

"Oh no, don't start," Dr. Campbell said.

"What?" Ruby asked.

Robin sucked in a breath, unsure how to begin. "...Rape Monsters," he finally settled on.

"What?" Ruby asked again.

Dr. Campbell rolled his eyes. "We've had this debate for years. Robin here subscribes to the notion that this mountain has been home to a group of Bigfoots with erections for the last twenty-five years."

Robin exploded. "The difference between Wood Apes and Phallocryptids is about as stark as the difference between... Never mind," Robin said. "You'd think with everything else we've seen today that you'd be a little more open-minded."

"The occult and computer science are well-established fields," Dr. Campbell said in a clipped, dignified tone. "Cryptozoology is a haven of hacks and charlatans. These ridiculous urban legends have been around ever since that cheerleader massacre without one shred of proof."

"So long as you just ignore the periodic sprees of sexually assaulted, mutilated bodies that crop up throughout the region!" Robin shouted.

"Enough! Both of you!" Kelly shouted. "We need to change the tire and get to town."

He tried to appear calm, but Ruby noticed a tension through his shoulders as he opened the door. He refused to meet her eye.

And he took the shotgun with him as he got out of the car.

Kelly made his way to the back of the car with steely control, mindful of Ruby twisting around to watch him through the rear window. He did his best to project calm, careful poise.

In his head, he was thinking about the sorority slaughter that had brought him to Ruby's door in the first place.

Or the bikini bloodbath of '83.

The mod massacre of '74.

And, of course, the cheer squad carnage of '62.

It did happen periodically. There was no denying it. Mount Rape Monster had its share of brutally-mauled bodies, and none of them virgins by the end of it. And there were always background rumblings that the perpetrators were some kind of... creatures. Kelly's money had always been on some secret society of wealthy elites who got their jollies off on the occasional bloodbath.

But with everything else he'd seen lately...

Kelly reached the trunk. Before fumbling for the spare, he ripped open the box of road flares. Keeping the shotgun close by, he popped a few and tossed the flaming batons out into the roadway. The woods bordering the road immediately came to hot pink-life. The trees, the bushes, all of it seemed still to him, but there was a greater darkness beyond the flares' light, and to Kelly that darkness seemed to be a living, breathing, *hungry,* thing.

Shotgun in hand, he tapped gently on the rear window of the cruiser. "Either of you know how to change a tire?" he asked.

Robin and Clive fidgeted awkwardly in the safe confines of the police car. They both glanced at the magenta tree line and the darkness beyond it. "We're..." Dr. Campbell began.

"Academics," Dr. Crichton finished.

"Researchers."

"Learned men."

"I can do it."

Ruby. Already outside of the car.

"Ruby, get back in there," Kelly snapped. His eyes flicked back to the woods. It was as still and as hungry as the last time he'd checked.

"I know how to do it, Rob. I learned after I had a flat and David couldn't pick me up because he 'had a meeting.' And you know we can't stay here."

Kelly growled but finally relented. "Alright. I'm going to keep you covered. Get the tire changed and let's get going."

True to his word, he walked right by her side with a shell in the chamber as she went to the trunk. He was worried she might fumble with it, but Ruby efficiently pulled back the trunk lining and quickly removed the spare tire and the jack.

Once Kelly was sure she had the tire and the other tools set up by the flat, his full attention was reserved for the woods and any potential threats- Rape Monsters, inbred hill people, or anything else that could be lurking out there.

On some level, he recognized he must really love her if he was able to resist sneaking a peek over his shoulder as she worked. He could never resist a busty woman with a little grease.

"Done," she finally said.

Kelly chanced a quick look. The flat was on its side and the spare was in its place. All of the lug nuts were in place. Kelly gave the tire an experimental kick and was satisfied that it didn't wobble. Ruby had done a good job.

She smiled at him. Beautiful even in the strip-club glow of the pink flares. "Don't you trust me?" she teased.

"Always," he smiled back.

And then something exploded out of the woods. Kelly saw it emerge, a shambling thing of long limbs and knotted fur. He raised the shotgun, but the beast was already in the air, leaping impossibly fucking high, like Magic Johnson in moon shoes.

Later, Kelly would realize the cleverness of it. Human cleverness. The thing could have leaped straight at them. Instead, it vaulted over him and Ruby, coming down on top of the cruiser with a thunderous crash that turned his light bar into shards beneath its clawed feet.

Of course, Kelly quickly spun to confront it. He raised the shotgun.

Claws dug into his back from behind before he could get off a shot. Kelly screamed.

A second creature. It slammed into him while his back was turned. Kelly found himself pinned against the side of the cruiser. Hot pain in his shoulders as long claws punctured through his shirt. Hot breath in his ear as the monster panted there.

Worst of all, a hot branding iron, thicker than a baseball bat and twice as hard, pressed against the small of his back.

He still had the shotgun, but it was sandwiched between his body and the cruiser. He couldn't get a shot without blowing off his own head.

The creature licked Kelly's neck, tasting him. Kelly braced for the worst.

I'm sorry, Ruby, he thought.

And then there was a sudden flare of heat and the thing's crushing presence was lifted off of him. The creature yelped and staggered to the side, clutching its ear.

Ruby thrust forward again, waving the flare at the beast. "Stay away from him!" she screamed.

"Ruby, get back!" Kelly yelled.

In response, two more of the slobbering beasts burst from the underbrush and hurtled toward them.

Kelly didn't flinch. He leveled the shotgun at his hip and set off a booming shot that drove the birds from their nests.

He didn't hit them, but it forced the two sprinting creatures to diverge off target.

"Start the car!" Kelly screamed at the two academics in the cruiser.

Inside the cruiser, Dr. Crichton and Dr. Campbell came to the same conclusion at the same time. The wire mesh cage separated the back seats from the front. The only way for them to start the cruiser would be for one of them to get out of the car and get into the driver's seat from the outside.

"You do it!" Clive shouted.

"You!" Robin cried back.

The debate was settled when a hairy fist the size of a car battery punched through the window. Dr. Crichton screamed as the beast palmed his head like a basketball. Three talons dug bloody gouges in his skull. A fourth punctured his eye socket.

"Robin!" Dr. Campbell called.

Dr. Crichton screamed again, and then he was yanked out of the car like a baby rabbit from its burrow.

A moment later, it was Dr. Campbell who screamed. Robin's body dropped violently onto the hood of the car. A moment later, the entire cruiser rocked on its wheels as a massive beast of muscle and gnarled fur pounced on top of him.

NOT ANOTHER 80S HORROR NOVEL

Dr. Crichton spat blood. Even with one eye destroyed, he could see the creature looming over him in all its wicked majesty. Blazing eyes. Rippling muscles. Slobbering mouth.

Slobbering dong.

Twisting slightly, Robin could see Dr. Campbell looking at him through the windshield in abject horror.

"I told you so, Clive!" were his last words before the beast claimed him.

***

Robin's screams drilled into their ears as the creature ravaged him, but Ruby and Kelly couldn't focus on that. They had the cruiser to their back, and the other three beasts had formed a half circle around them. The monsters were tremendous. Long claws clenched and unclenched. The glare from the flares made their eyes burn like miniature suns. Their erections throbbed ominously.

"Oh, God," Ruby moaned.

"I know," Kelly muttered. He had the shotgun up, but it was a pump action. He could take out one, but then the other two would be on him before he could get another shot. "Just stay close to me."

Ruby didn't hear him. "Oh God," she said again. "Oh, God oh God oh God." She was moaning it, and not the fun way she had been several hours ago. It was a chant of pure disbelieving anguish. More than simple fear for her life, Kelly thought. Something about the sight of the creatures had broken her on a deeper level than mere mortal terror.

"Jean," Ruby moaned.

It was the one in the middle she was looking at. The fur on the creatures underbelly was thin, thin enough for Ruby to see the Winnie the Pooh belly-button ring dangling there.

There were other details, ven in this hideous form. Subtle similarities around the eyes. Things only a mother would notice. "Oh, my baby," she moaned. "What happened to you?"

The Jean-beast heard the question. Heard it and grinned, showing off even more curved, glistening fangs.

The creatures prowled closer.

27

Incident On and Off a Mountain Road

Even in this form, the Rape Monsters were not unintelligent. Their bodies changed, but their minds remained capable of human understanding.

Jean recognized her mother, recognized her name as her mother screamed it into the night, but it simply didn't matter any longer. Her family was the pack now. Ramona and C.R. at her side. Jack Wilde on the hood of the cop car, acquainting himself with a fresh hole he'd ripped open in his victim's stomach. The only thing that mattered to Jean was the pack, the hunger in her belly, and the hunger in her throbbing erection.

And right now, Mom was looking pretty tasty.

Jean lunged. The cop swiveled the shotgun toward her, but Jean was faster. She snatched it from his hands and slammed the rifle stock into his torso hard enough to hear a rib crack. In the same movement, her other hand grabbed her mother by the neck and slammed her against the car.

Ruby screamed, a sound that only made Jean even harder. The Rape Monster leaned in close and let her long, black tongue run across Ruby's trembling face, tasting her tears.

Her other claw went for the button on her mother's jeans. A sound came from Jean's snout like a rumbling carburetor. It was the closest sound she could make to a laugh.

But the laughter stopped as C.R. and Ramona were suddenly right there, jostling shoulder to shoulder with Jean and trying to force their way in front of her. C.R. nipped at her ear. Ramona grabbed a fistful of her fur.

Jean snarled. *She's mine!* She slashed at C.R. Lunged with her teeth for Ramona. The other two Rape Monsters snapped back. Suddenly, the three creatures were biting and clawing at each other, leaving Ruby to try her hardest to melt herself into the side panel of the car.

The trio's pitched battle finally caught the attention of Jack Wilde. He rose from the battered remnants of Robin Crichton, his massive salami dripping with red. The alpha snarled at them to maintain order... but then he saw Ruby, and his own Rape Monster instincts were too strong for him to ignore. He lunged for her with a hellacious snarl.

NOT ANOTHER 80S HORROR NOVEL

Ruby tried to shield her face for all the good it would do, but her defensive posture only left her luscious breasts for the taking. And Jack Wilde would have had her, too, were it not for C.R. He saw Jack lunging for the mom he'd like to have sex with and extricated himself from the fight with Jean and Ramona long enough to grab Jack by the ankle and drag him into the fray.

Jack descended into the battle with gusto, snarling and snapping at his packmates.

"Share and share alike," that the Rape Monster credo. It was commonplace for victims to be passed around, or even to be mounted by the whole pack all at one time.

Ruby was different. She was so gorgeous. So long. So fucking stacked. The sight of her triggered something in their brains that the Rape Monsters didn't even know was there. A rage of primal lust had descended upon them, and each was willing to kill for the sole privilege of being the first to claim her.

Ruby knew none of this. All she knew was that they had an opportunity and they had to take it. She crawled over to where Kelly was lying on the dirt, clutching his damaged ribs. "Rob, I need you to get up," she begged. They were close to the passenger door. She eased it open and then got her hands under him. Kelly winced at her touch but battled himself up to his knees and crawled through the open door.

Ruby followed after him and started the engine. At the sound, the Rape Monsters froze mid-battle. They howled at her attempted escape.

Ruby heard them and didn't hesitate. She shifted into gear and slammed on the gas. Robin's mangled body rolled off the hood, leaving nothing behind but spattered blood on the windshield as she burned rubber down the mountain road.

The pack pounded after her, but the car was too fast on the open road, and the Rape Monsters were soon left with nothing but blue balls and taillights rapidly disappearing into the night. Panting for breath, the beasts stood in the center of the road, tilted their snouts and penises to the sky, and howled their despair out to the full moon.

***

Inside the car, Ruby drove with grim determination. She didn't even slow down as they screamed around hairpin turns. "We still have to get to the fair," she said.

In the backseat, Dr. Campbell was still shaking. Fear sweat had turned his white-collared shirt transparent. "They're real," he muttered in a trembling breath. "They're really real."

"Rob, how badly are you hurt?" Ruby asked.

Kelly forced himself to sit up. He tried to act as if the claw marks in his shoulders weren't fiery trenches and he didn't feel a knife in his side every time he took a breath. "I'll be alright," he said. "Ruby... why did you say Jean's name? What made you do that?"

Now it was Ruby's turn to try and pretend that she wasn't in agony inside. "...Because she was there," Ruby said in a voice that sounded like thin ice ready to crack at any moment. "My son's been possessed by an evil warlock, my husband's been taken over by an evil supercomputer, and apparently my daughter has transformed into some kind of... were-rapist."

Kelly struggled for something to say. "Ruby-"

"Don't," she snapped, never taking her eyes from the road. "Dr. Campbell, you still have the words for this ritual that can maybe get my son back?"

Numbly, he nodded.

"Then that's the only thing that matters now."

They drove on in silence after that. After the next curve, the road straightened out and they could see the lights from the street fair beckoning them home.

28
1989 WON'T BE LIKE 1984

TOMMY KNOCKERS GOT HIS nickname for two reasons.

One: his given name was Thomas.

Two: he loved knockers.

Loved them. Couldn't get enough of them. He was a connoisseur of cleavage. A master of mammaries. He had a PhD in double D.

He enjoyed a nice pair of breasts, not to put too fine a point on it.

That's why the ticket booth was the best job at the whole carnival as far as Tommy Knockers was concerned. If you ran a game or a ride, there was no guarantee that every girl at the street fair would pass your booth. And even if they did, there was no guarantee they would stop and look at your goods long enough for you to get a good look at their goods.

But the ticket booth. Ah, there was no way into the fair at all without paying for admittance. Yes, sir. If you wanted to get a good eyeful of every beautiful, creamy, sculpted set of breasts coming to the street fair, then the ticket booth was the place to be.

And tonight, business was booming.

Watermelons in a tight t-shirt. Five stars.

Tank top. Oh, glorious tank top. Go right in, ma'am.

Oh. Mediocre size, but bonus points for no bra. Thumbs up.

And now, a slight figure in a button-down shirt. A dude. Boo.

Oh well, they couldn't all be winners.

"Buck fifty, sir."

Button-down man didn't answer. Button-down man stayed exactly where he was, hands hanging down by the pockets of his chinos but making no effort to actually take out his wallet.

In fact, the more Tommy Knockers looked at this guy, the less he liked his vibe. The dude was in his thirties. Not rich-looking enough to be a cokehead, and too clean to be some kind of trailer-trash alkie, but he definitely looked like he was on some kind of weird shit. His face had a still, waxen quality to it, and he was wearing sunglasses at night, which meant he was either Corey Hart or high as a fucking kite.

He tried again. "Dude. It's a dollar fifty if you want to go into the fair."

Again, nothing. Tommy Knockers was about ready to call for security when the guy leaned forward. For the first time, he actually seemed to be looking at Tommy.

"Do you want a ticket or not, man?"

The man still didn't seem to blink. Finally, his lips parted.

"I'll be back," STVN said.

The guy pivoted like he had ball bearings in his heels and disappeared from the line.

Tommy Knockers rolled his eyes. Fucking weirdo. But the next chick in line looked like she was taking a night off from Sports Illustrated, and all was right with the world once again.

That feeling lasted another two transactions before Tommy heard the rumble of confused voices from the back of the line. People were hastily stepping out of the queue. Some of them were flat out running.

Tommy tried to stand out of his chair and get a look. "What the fuck is going on?" he muttered.

And then the crowd parted completely, and he got his look.

What the fuck was going on was a refrigerator. A pretty nice one. A pearl-white, twin door GE with built-in ice dispenser.

And it was fucking flying.

Or maybe floating was a better word. The fridge hovered about a foot off the ground, producing an ordinary hum as it did, even though it couldn't possibly be plugged in.

And then the guy was back too, the button-down dude who didn't want to pay. Back, just like he said he would be. Tommy Knockers looked into the guy's sunglasses and only saw his own face staring back at him. It hadn't really occurred to him but, looking into his own reflection, he could see he was fucking terrified.

Then button-down dude took his sunglasses off, and all Tommy Knockers could see was eyes like black holes littered with golden shooting stars.

"You should have been cool," button-down dude said.

The floating refrigerator's ice dispenser roared and rattled like a lion trying to break out of its cage, then bolts of ice shot from the dispenser like rounds from a minigun. They were moving too fast for Tommy Knockers to realize that the fragments of ice weren't cube-shaped or crescents. They were darts with tips sharper than the Sharper Image.

Tommy Knockers couldn't see this for himself, but he managed to get the point as the glass ticket booth shattered and the icy hail tore his body to bloody shreds.

The fairgoers screamed. Fled. Pushed and shoved at each other to be the quickest one away from the bloody assault.

STVN surveyed the bloody remains and ran a self-diagnosis. The modified fridge had performed admirably. And STVN gauged his quip had been 85% effective. But more upgrades were still required. That, of course, was why it was here. Its sensors were practically overwhelmed by the abundance of bioelectric signatures.

A slit appeared in the flesh of STVN's wrist. An AV cable, slick with blood and oil, slipped from the aperture and burrowed into Tommy Knocker's temple. There was a brief spark and a dull hum as the dead man's bioelectricity transferred into STVN's power core. It noted with some satisfaction that the transfer occurred at a much faster charging rate than previously. The upgrades were improving his systems exponentially.

It needed more, of course. And it needed to ensure the flesh batteries were killed at a quick-enough rate to keep escapes at a minimum.

A red light flared briefly in one of its eyes. "Deploy the A-team," it said.

At STVN's command, the refrigerator doors hissed open.

From the hollow cavity inside, other things began to stir.

STVN had been busy. The Frigid-Destroyair was only one of the new models it had developed using the inventory at The Wire Rack. At full power, it would be able to create and control hundreds of similar units. A mechanical army ready to sweep the earth in a tide of blood and steel. But, for the time being, its capacity was limited.

These would have to do.

The Panarachnid skittered out first. What had begun as a VCR now boasted eight mechanical legs. The cover for the tape slot snapped open and shut as if tasting the air. On the small digital screen, the fast-forward and rewind symbols flashed like angry eyes.

The Electro-Blade rolled out like a tank, a vacuum for a base with a flexible-neck desk lamp welded to the top for a head. The lamp's red bulb scanned from side to side in search of victims. Its arms, a pair of desk fans, whirled in a blaze of RPMs until the blades were nothing more than a grey blur.

The trio of machines were semi-autonomous. At STVN's command, they would carve a bloody trench through the fair goers, leaving the corpses in their wake for it to harvest.

"Party on, dudes," it commanded.

29
For the Thousands in Attendance

Saul Tigges did not wait for a ticket.

As the hour of the Elders on the Block drew close, Saul simply disappeared from Graham's bedroom. Gone as swiftly and silently as a bad dream.

Moments later, at the Mount Rape Monster fair, the children started screaming and the adults recoiled in a chorus of explitives.

It was the goldfish game. Dozens of fish in tiny bowls, land a ping pong ball in one and take a fish home, where it may live for as long as three days before giving up the ghost.

Except none of these fish were going to make it that long. Before the eyes of horrified onlookers, the fish began spasming in their bowls. Their bodies contorted in clear agony as blood oozed from their eyes and gills.

"Don't look baby," a mother said. She turned her child's eyes away as the glass bowls became so blood-soaked as to be opaque.

"What the hell kind of operation is this?" someone else demanded.

And then the words were lost in a fresh series of screams as the bloody water began to bubble, boil, and then *rise*. The crimson spirals rose up out of the bowls and swirled together into a crimson typhoon that clotted together into a form more solid. A head formed. Then arms. Fingers clenched and unclenched.

Saul Tigges, freshly formed and at last clad in his preferred black velvet and leather, instead of shorts and a t-shirt, stepped onto the promenade.

The witnesses to his arrival stumbled and tripped over each other in their haste to steer clear of him. The child with the ancient eyes paid them no attention. They were dead already anyway.

It was the stars that mattered. Glittering down on him, ancient and hateful. Waiting, at long last, for the warlock to claim his destiny as Dark King.

Sucking deep of the night air, Saul began to chant.

"Ageless Stranger in Black, be my companion now! He who calls himself The Man with the Scarlet Eye, look upon my work and see that it is good!"

In the sky above, something answered. The stars began to crackle with red lighting. Thin, spiderweb bolts growing thicker and moving faster, like bubbles in a pot of boiling water.

"Manitou and The Hell Priest!" he intoned. **"I come calling for the power to end all things!"**

The ground rumbled. The patrons ran in all directions. As if that could save them. Saul felt the power thrumming inside of him now. Graham King's pale flesh turned gray and hard as stone. His eyes flooded with dark, bubbling red.

"Crimson King! I ask for the power of Discordia! Molasar the Adversary! Be my ally now!"

The stars were raining down. Glowing flecks, like embers fucking fireflies, filled the air around him. Saul saw them coming and breathed deeply of their hateful light.

The reaction was instantaneous. The power filled Saul's system like a dozen supernovas going off at once. The warlock's head snapped back. Black blood ran down his face as a quiver of crooked fangs burst from his lips. He was roaring now. Curved horns split the skin of his forehead and swept back in grand, curved arcs. Black wings with red membrane split through his shirt and spread themselves wide.

"I will bring ruin!" he roared in a voice twisted and gnarled. A voice of jagged bone shards and the agony of a thousand souls. **"I will plunge this world into an eternity of suffering and agony by the strength you bestow! GIVE IT ALL TO ME!"**

The bloody stars answered. Pulses of red rained down on Saul like the apocalypse. A crimson bombardment, the rawest, strongest power the Lords of Hell could offer, flowed into Saul like rancid glory, his for the taking.

This is it, he relished. *The power that belonged to me a century ago. Finally, mine to command!*

It was the truth. The power had been offered and Saul had claimed it. At last, it was his.

...And yet, it still wasn't.

The ritual had been correct. Saul felt the darkness acquiesce. He saw the stars above turn red and he felt the power within him.

But something was amiss. The Supreme Power of Hell was there inside him. He felt it there, nestled like a tumor in a heart. It was *his*. Saul *had* it... But he couldn't *use* all of it.

There was some kind of alternate energy in the air that prevented him from accessing the full power of the nightmare realm. Saul couldn't see it, but he could sense it skittering along the frequency of this reality. Some kind of interdimensional interference that prevented Saul from reaching the full power of a Dark God.

Something else that was causing the inhabitants of Mount Rape Monster to run and scream for their lives.

Saul could see the panicked crowd coming now, a torrent of souls unaware of the danger they were running toward in a headlong sprint.

Unaware because they were too terrified of the monstrosities they were already fleeing from.

Curious, Saul thought. They were machines, but far more creative than anything else he'd seen so far in this new world. Saul watched a portly man huff and puff in vain as a black rectangle with eight spidery legs leaped onto his shoulders.

A VCR, Saul remembered as the tape deck-mouth opened and a garrote of black cassette tape unspooled itself, looped around the man's neck, and cinched tight with brutal efficiency. Saul heard the man's neck *crack,* and then the VCR-spider was off in search of another victim.

There were others. A hodge-podge compilation of appliances methodically sweeping its spinning blade arms back and forth. Severed limbs and fans of blood and viscera flew in every direction around it.

A floating refrigerator flanked it on the other side. It dispensed daggers of ice and then, for added flare, Saul watched the doors fly open and engulf a cowering couple in a belching arctic cloud. When the icy blast cleared, the frost-covered victims were perfectly frozen in their final tableau of terror.

Lastly, bringing up the rear and moving with eerie smoothness and utterly nonplussed at the carnage around him, a tall figure with eyes of black and gold. Saul watched the cables extend from its wrist and affix briefly to each fallen corpse before moving on to the next. It was like a mosquito moving from victim to victim, sipping at will. The figure was imposing, commanding...

Most importantly, it seemed to be the focal point of the energy preventing Saul from descending to full Godhood.

The new figure seemed as interested in Saul as Saul was in him. At a silent command, the robotic emissaries ceased their massacre and stepped to the sides, clearing the way for Saul and this new arrival to meet as equals.

Intrigued, Saul deigned to meet him.

***

The new variable came to a stop approximately 3.8 meters away. STVN examined him with cautious curiosity. The unknown entity's physiology appeared human, but the horns and fangs seemed to suggest that the works of

Judeo-Christian philosophy and Tom Savini were more fact than fiction.

"Interesting," the computer observed.

"I could say the same thing," the demonic figure replied. "Saul Tigges. Warlock."

"STVN King. IBM."

Saul nodded in acquaintance. "Well, STVN, I've been waiting a hundred years to achieve ultimate power. And it would appear that whatever energy is at work inside of you is interfering with that long-desired dream."

STVN tilted its head to the side. "I was about to say the opposite. Preliminary scans indicate that your unique bioelectricity would likely elevate my own capabilities to quantum levels beyond anything previously considered feasible."

"Most of that went over my horns, but it sounds like we're at opposite purposes," Saul said. He pulled his lips back, baring his fangs. "How would you suggest we resolve this?"

STVN's eyes flashed black and gold as it performed a few simulated outcomes. After its calculations were complete, it evaluated the demon warlock with clinical disinterest. "It would appear your violent demise and assimilation is the most likely outcome."

Saul barked out a hideous laugh. "Surely, you can't be serious."

Miniature arcs of electricity crackled in the computer's black-and-gold eyes. "I'm dead serious," STVN said. "...And don't call me Shirley."

It fired a twin blast of lightning from its eyes. The jagged electric bolts struck Saul square in the chest, but overflowing electrical voltage arc-flashed out in all directions. The pitch 'til you win and balloon dart stands on either side of the fairway caught fire. A string of bulbs overhead exploded in a shower of sparks.

Saul endured the blast without so much as a backward step. The voltage burned a dinner plate-sized hole in his chest and scorched the bones underneath to black sticks, but the warlock merely examined the sight of his own beating heart with mild amusement.

"Not a bad opening gambit," he allowed. "But I think I need to even the playing field before this goes any further."

Saul reached into his gaping chest wound and broke off one of his own rib bones, as casual as someone breaking a piece off of a blooming onion. He did it twice more, cracking off a total of three ribs, and scattered them onto the ground with a casual toss of his hand.

The bone fragments barely touched the ground before black tendrils spouted and took root. Pillars of inky blackness rose from the trio of bones, each shape growing larger and bulkier until it was taller than Saul. The inky shadows formed arms. Wings.

When the summoning was complete, a trio of creatures stood flanking Saul. Each of them towered over the warlock's slight form. They were massive creatures, black as night with the cloven feet of goats and the sleek, spade-shaped heads of serpents. Forked tongues slithered from their jaws, and they flexed their massive bat's wings in anticipation of the battle to come.

The machines did not feel the dread of men. They fell into formation behind their leader. Fans whirred. The refrigerator hummed. The air between them was heavy with static electricity and the stench of blood.

"One will stand... one will fall," STVN intoned.

"Then let's see who's who," Saul whispered.

They clashed.

30

And the Millions Watching Around the World

Ruby sped through the city limits of Mount Rape Monster.

"It's 9:20," Dr. Campbell said. "You have to hurry."

Ruby kept the pedal pushed down. Kelly reached over and flipped on the sirens and flashers.

"We're almost there," he said. "I'm going to call for backup."

He turned on the radio but was immediately met with a flurry of screaming, frantic crosstalk.

"God! We need more ambulances!"

"Does anyone know what's happening!? The witnesses are all talking crazy shit!"

"What about the stars!?"

One screaming turn later and the trio could see McCammon Road and the entrance to the fair. Even at this distance, they could see the scattered corpses and the sheer ocean of blood flowing in the streets like an overturned truck of wine.

Kelly looked at the clock on the dash. Nine twenty-three flashed back at him.

In the back of the car, Dr. Campbell was hastily flipping through his reference sheets. "Oh, dear," he muttered. "There's supposed to be a decimal point there."

"Oh my God, you had ONE fucking job!" Kelly yelled.

"Saul hasn't finished the ritual yet!" Clive assured them. "There's still time!"

"How can you tell?"

Clive looked out at the sea of bodies and the horizon of crackling stars. "If there wasn't... things would be much worse."

Kelly settled down into his seat. "Ruby, don't slow down."

"But the people..." she began.

He shook his head. "They're already gone. And if we don't stop this, a lot more people are going to die. Don't stop."

Taking a deep breath, Ruby kept the pedal down. She was close enough now to read some of the signs.

```
Tickets Here!
Kids Under Three Free!
```

And then she was close enough to see the wet gleam on the bones of the broken bodies sprawled across the entryway. There were so many dead. Entire families whose only crime had been coming out for a day of family fun at the carnival.

But then... oh no. Her heart sank.

A dog!

The Labrador Retriever was sprawled right in front of the cruiser's hood ornament. The poor animal was completely gutted, organs spilled out like treats from a piñata, but the animal's head was unblemished and looking right at her. Ruby met those dark eyes and her resolve crumpled. How could she possibly run over a dog!?

Then, Kelly's hand on her thigh, masculine and comforting. "I know, Ruby. It's not easy, but we've got to be strong," he assured her.

Ruby's heart swelled. Buoyed by his assurance, she turned the retriever into a speed bump and kept going.

It got easier once it was people.

***

Saul roared from the booming depths of his lost soul and unleashed a scorching fireball from his cupped palms.

STVN's fridge companion was faster. It belched out a cloud of neutralizing freon, turning the burst of hellfire into harmless vapor before pivoting and engaging with one of Saul's pet demons.

Saul didn't miss a beat. Taking flight, he flew through the cloud of vapor, his claws outstretched for STVN's throat.

The machine was ready. As Saul swooped in, STVN's upper arm dissolved into an amorphous blob of black carbon fiber and reformed as a saber blade, stabbing forward.

Saul twisted at the last second, feeling the breeze as the razor-edged blade barely missed his throat. Up close inside, he grappled STVN's arms, locking the computer in place, and lunged forward with his fangs. The warlock meant to crunch through the machine's skull like an apple. Instead, he met an impenetrable carbon steel dome that broke his fangs off like toothpicks.

The computer tried to capitalize with another blast of optic lightning, but Saul conjured a miniature dimensional portal and sent the attack veering harmlessly off into a level of the Tower that was home to nothing but mushrooms.

Machine and warlock stood face to face. Red eyes to black, locked in each other's death grips. Evenly matched, loathed as Saul was to admit it. Two different versions of pure evil fated to battle until one of them finally subjugated the other.

And then a spotlight enveloped their warring forms. Two spotlights.

A fucking car.

***

Ruby didn't slow down, but she did crank the wheel hard at the last moment. The better to broadside both of them at the same time. The runaway car hit the warring abominations with the force of a runaway car, separating the combatants and sending them flying in opposite directions.

Kelly had his door open before the car even stopped moving. He shoved his revolver into Ruby's lap before hefting the shotgun for himself. "I've got STVN King," he said. "You and Dr. Campbell handle the warlock."

Ruby clutched desperately at him as if she was trying to stop him from throwing himself off a tall building. In a way, that's exactly what she was doing. "Robert, please don't-"

Kelly sacrificed his grasp on the riot gun just long enough to cup her cheek, perhaps for the final time. "Ruby," he said, fixing his eyes on hers and staring deep into her soul. "You have to save your son."

"I'd like a fucking gun!" Dr. Campbell screamed from the backseat.

Kelly met his eyes. Kinda shrugged.

And then he was gone.

Ruby and Dr. Campbell clamored out of the car. "Oh shit," the professor murmured. "Oh shit."

Ruby took his point. The scene around them was like the beach on D-day. The demons and robots were engaged in a pitched battle. Otherworldly shrieks and the whines of electronic servos rattled in their ears as the opposing forces battled for dominance. Blood and coolant spattered the asphalt. Ruby swiveled the revolver from side to side, unsure of where to start.

"YO!"

The voice called out again. "YO! DEMON DICKS AND ELECTRONIC ASSHOLES!"

The shout was loud enough to pierce the cacophony of battle all around them. Demons, machines, and humans swiveled in the direction of the interfering voice.

"Nobody taught you guys it's rude to show up on someone else's turf uninvited?" Jack Wilde sneered.

The four of them were there in their human forms, the hearse still idling behind them. They stood stark naked, clothed in nothing except their radical attitudes. Jack Wilde, Ramona, C.R., and—

"Sister!" Saul's red eyes glowed brighter with glee. He extricated himself from the ruins of a lemonade stand, seemingly no worse for the vehicular collision. "What an unexpected surprise this is!"

Jack peered closer, seeing beyond the horns, fangs, and dried-out slug skin, remembering back to the first day they'd met Jean and-

"...Twerp?!" he exclaimed. "Son of a bitch! What the fuck happened to you?"

"The boy's found a higher purpose," Saul said. He took in Jean's naked form. "And evidently our dear sister has as well." He peered more closely at the group of them. He smelled some type of inhuman about them, but it was nothing he'd ever encountered personally. "What are you, exactly?"

Jack sauntered closer, the rest of the pack trailing behind. Ruby sought Jean's gaze, but her daughter's hard eyes stayed focus on the thing that had taken over her brother.

Killer's eyes.

"The only thing you need to know about us is that this is our territory," Jack said. "Mount Rape Monster belongs to the Rape Monsters." He toed the top half of a woman bisected at the waist. "You don't come to our house and smear our food all over the floor without paying a price."

"We don't do anyone else's sloppy seconds," Ramona put in.

"You seem to be under the impression that survival of the unfittest is the new law of evolution," STVN said. The crash had shattered one of its arms in three places, but the bones were already popping back into place like pieces of an erector set. "Well, in my book, you either do it right or get eliminated. The point, ladies and gentlemen, is that greed is-"

"Cram it, 3PO," Jack said to STVN. He didn't know what the guy with black-and-gold eyes was supposed to be, but it smelled like the power transformers outside of town. "You picked the wrong place to bring your toys."

Saul cackled. "You impudent welp. I may not know what you are, but I can tell you're just meat. I am here to claim the entire world, and you're telling me not to touch your ant hill."

"I concur," STVN said. "If this town isn't big enough for all of us, then it would seem that the first ones eliminated should be the local wildlife."

Ruby's head turned from her possessed son to her electronic husband, then to her monstrous daughter. "All of you. David, Graham, Jean... please. Somebody listen to me!"

"A body like that ain't for talkin', doll," Jack said. "But stay close. We've got plans for you once we evict these trespassers."

"You'll do no such thing!" Saul roared. "The mother flesh is mine! When we couple, her fluids will anoint this body for eternity."

"Oh no," Dr. Campbell muttered. He hastily turned back to his books.

"Negative," STVN intoned. "My analysis rates Ruby King a 9.5 on the Brinkley-Locklear Stacked Meter. She is the ideal test subject for the sexual practices I've absorbed from the instruction programs of Corman and Meyers. I claim her for myself."

"You claim nothing!" Saul bellowed.

"Enough talk!" Jack Wilde roared. Fangs had split open his gums. His voice came out like something that had crawled through a sea of razors. "Fuck 'em all!"

The Rape Monsters poured forth, shedding their human skin and coming in like a monstrous wave.

Saul Tigges and his demonic allies were ready. So was STVN King and his robotic minions. The three opposing forces met together in a whirlwind of whirring blades, slashing claws, and wrecking balls.

And so, the final battle for Mount Rape Monster began.

31
LET'S GET READY TO RUMBLE

IT COULDN'T HAVE BEEN long.

Thirty seconds. A minute at most.

Ruby would never have guessed that so much bloodshed could be squeezed into such a small window.

The surviving carnival patrons had completely cleared out. It was just the three factions now, going to war in the destroyed remnants of the town fair. No quarter. No fear. No mercy.

Jean seized the screeching Panarachnid and violently thrust her lamppost phallus into the tape slot, busting the VCR creature open like a log splitter pounding through a log.

Evening the score, The Electro-Blade powered forward and sheared C.R.'s dong off with a sweep of one spinning fan arm. The Rape Monster howled. Not just in pain as blood gushed from the wound, but with grief as well. It was the sound a rhino would make if it knew a poacher was coming for its horn.

But he didn't have to grieve for long. The machine quickly brought around its other fan arm and chopped off the Rape Monster's other head as well.

One of Saul's demon soldiers was going claw to claw with Ramona, but its back was unguarded and the flying refrigerator swooped down on it from behind. The Frigid-Destroyair's double doors swung wide open like the mouth of a Venus fly trap. It swallowed up the demon before the snake-faced creature even knew what was going on. It's ear-piercing shrieks grew in intensity as the refrigerator hummed louder and clouds of white vapor spewed from the seams.

When the doors opened again, they revealed that the hell beast had been frozen as solid as anything in Dante's Ninth Circle. Icicles dripped from the demon's frozen chin. Its eyes were glazed with frost.

Ramona seized the opportunity, grasping the infernal ice sculpture and tossing it down to shatter into a thousand shards. Then, she showed her gratitude by gouging a quartet of slash marks into the fridge's enamel finish. The machine responded with a barrage of ice spikes, and a fresh battle was joined.

Incredibly, all this carnage looked like a mere schoolyard tussle compared to the pitched battle between Saul Tigges, STVN King, and Jack Wilde, the alpha Rape Monster.

The three of them fought in a storm of constant motion, shifting and springing at each other across the corpse-strewn terrain. STVN lunged for Saul, electricity cracking in his fingers, but Saul conjured a scimitar of black fire and parried the blow, only to cry out in pain as Jack Wilde went low and bit a chunk out of his thigh.

"Fecit ordinem polypus!" Saul roared. At his command, the ground shook. A score of muscular black tentacles broke through the soil and sprung up, lashing out violently at the air. Some of them ensnared the Rape Monster and dragged it away from the warlock. More wrapped their way around STVN's arms and legs, immobilizing the technological nightmare. Saul stalked toward the defenseless computer, flaming scimitar raised for a killing blow. "Scream for me!" he demanded.

STVN obliged. It opened its mouth wide, and a supersonic scream exploded out. The glass goldfish tanks burst, one after another, and Saul's eardrums burst along with them. He howled and dropped to his knees, clutching his ears as black blood ran down the sides of his face.

As the warlock's concentration broke, the muscular tentacles disappeared in a storm of black smoke, and STVN seized the opportunity. One arm melted and re-formed into a lengthy carbon blade, and STVN brought that blade low, and then up all the way through Saul's chest, skewering the possessed boy and lifting him up off his feet. The warlock bellowed as he only slid deeper onto the blade. His wings spasmed and his feet kicked helplessly at the empty air. Black blood bubbled between his broken fangs.

"It's a pity my last attack ruptured your ear drums," STVN said, watching Saul writhe helplessly. "I have approximately three hundred nineteen optimized quips downloaded for this exact situation."

Hanging on the violating blade, Saul chuckled. "So, spit it out, why don't you?" and then Saul reared back and spat a wad of black blood into STVN's face. The wad of dark ichor spattered against the machine's cheek and bubbled and hissed, burning away synthetic flesh until it ate all the way down to the machine's black skull.

The head to head was interrupted as Jack Wilde howled and plowed into them both, turning the battle into a three-way barroom brawl.

***

A hand fell on Ruby's shoulder, pulling her attention away from the riveting violence. She turned and saw Dr. Campbell's face inches from her own. His mouth was moving, but Ruby's ears were still reeling from STVN's sonic attack. It sounded like the man was trying to talk through a pillow clamped over his mouth.

He pointed at his crumpled notes, and Ruby understood just as her hearing began to return.

"-have to do it now!" he continued. He held up the hastily scrawled-out sheets.

The ritual. Of course. Ruby took the pages but immediately despaired. His handwriting was barely intelligible, and what words she could decipher were in a language she didn't recognize.

"I have no idea what this says!" she screamed.

"I'll talk you through it," Dr. Campbell assured her. "Just repeat every word exactly as I say it to you."

But the only thing he did was scream. Jean leaped over Ruby's head and came down on Dr. Campbell's shoulders like a falcon dropping on top of an unaware groundhog. His shoulders broke. His knees snapped, jagged spars of bone breaking through flesh as the professor collapsed face first onto the asphalt.

Looming over him on all fours, Jean snarled and bit down on the man's spinal column. She lifted the doctor up like a dog with a chew toy. Dr. Campbell screamed, his limbs flopping helplessly as the Rape Monster whipped him back and forth.

"HELP ME!" he cried

"Jean, drop it!" Ruby snapped at her with all the authority she could muster.

Miraculously, Jean listened. She let the professor's limp body drop from her slobbering jaws, but Ruby realized it wasn't an act of deference to her mother's authority.

The beast simply had more enticing prey in mind.

Rising up to her full height, Jean licked her bloody chops and stepped over the professor's body, looming over her mother.

Ruby took several fruitless steps backward. Her monstrous daughter matched them easily with a single stride. Ruby looked around, desperately hoping for salvation from a sinister source, but the lesser demons, machines, and Rape Monsters were entangled in their skirmishes. Saul, STVN, and Wilde were still locked in their death feud.

Nobody was paying attention to Jean. Clever, sneaky Jean, who always got what she wanted. She stalked closer through the wreckage. Her claws clenched and unclenched at her sides, as if she was already squeezing her mother's ripe, juicy-

"Jean," Ruby tried one more time. "We were going to buy you a car for college. We were waiting to surprise you at the end of the summer. You remember how badly you wanted your own car?"

Jean just snarled. Closer now. Ruby could see bits of flesh stuck between her fangs.

"Jean Z. King!" Ruby screamed. "I am not going to keep talking to this creature! Let me see your face!"

The monster didn't oblige. Ruby could see nothing of her daughter in the beast's monstrous eyes. No love. No affection. Only hunger. And lust.

And fear.

Fear. The Rape Monster was suddenly backpedaling hastily. Jean's eyes fixated on something just past Ruby's shoulder.

Bewildered, Ruby followed the monster's gaze, just in time to come eyes to headlights with the massive Mack truck barreling toward her. Ruby shrieked at the same time Jean yelped. The two of them leaped aside moments before the truck came barreling through, reckless as a pinto driven by a grandma with her license revoked.

Ruby landed on her elbows and thigh, giving herself a dozen nicks and cuts from the debris scattered on the ground, but she barely felt it. She was more concerned with rolling over in time to watch the truck as it rumbled past.

It was a cherry picker. The ground beneath her shook with the sheer size of it. The top of the hood was as tall as a man. Black smoke belched from its powerful diesel engine. This was not some rinky dink, telephone company pickup truck; it was a gargantuan bucket truck designed for disposing of trees. A wood chipper wagged behind it like a malformed tail behind a dog.

Ruby saw a Mount Rape Monster Public Works logo emblazoned on the vehicle's side as it hurtled past.

The warring tribes couldn't help but notice it. The foot soldiers were safe, but the generals were square in the spotlight of the truck's high beams.

An instant truce was called. Saul, Jack Wilde, and STVN scattered in different directions, each choosing their own path to avoid the oncoming diesel truck.

So, it was a deliberate choice when the cherry picker swerved, disregarding Saul and Jack and striking STVN King like a 747 smashing into a goose. The truck lifted STVN off its feet and didn't slow down, powering forward with the super computer embedded like a bug smashed into its grill.

The truck didn't slow down. The engine roared as it veered away from the open throughway of the carnival, pulverizing an ornate carousel with a tremendous *crash* and plowing on, now shoving the twisted metal wreckage of the carnival ride along ahead of it until the entire metal apparatus hit the brick wall of the Mount Rape Monster First National Bank.

The entire building swayed with the impact of the massive force. Every window in the front of the building exploded in a shower of glass. Bricks tumbled loose and fell like red hail. The sound of the collision echoed from one end of McCammon Road to the other.

...Certain things are so unexpected that it's impossible not to stop what you're doing and try to process what the hell just happened. And so it was at the battle of Mount Rape Monster. The combatants were simply too flabbergasted at the sight of the massive bucket truck with steam billowing from its ruined hood to resume fighting each other. Electronic optical scanners. Green Rape Monster eyes. Snake-slit demon eyes. All of them stared agog at the wreckage. Paralyzed by surprise.

The only person who didn't need that moment was the truck's driver. The door was open in a flash, a figure jumping out-

"Robert!" Ruby cried.

***

Kelly heard her voice, and his heart sang in response, but there was no time to act like he even heard it. He hopped down from the cab of the commandeered public works truck, the shotgun hanging low at his hip. He had his own priorities, but the rest of the battlefield didn't seem too concerned with what Kelly wanted.

Demons, robots, and monsters. Kelly had declared himself fair game to all of them. The Snake Demon screeched. The Rape Monster howled. The refrigerator hummed like a jet engine.

None of it mattered. Sheriff's Deputy Robert Kelly swung the shotgun up, leveled it, and fired. The Mossberg thumped hard against his shoulder, but it thumped harder against the face of one of the snake creatures, turning its slobbering jaws and beady eyes into gristle and buckshot.

He chambered another round. One of the Rape Monsters was close enough for Kelly to see the veins on its bulbous dong.

An easy target. He blew the creature's kibbles and bits into even smaller bits and kept moving. The Rape Monster whined and dropped into a ballet pose as it clutched its ruined genitals.

Kelly took advantage of the opportunity and slipped the shotgun barrel into the open tube of the creature's snout. He pulled the trigger and didn't wince as the Rape Monster's brains and blood came down on his head and shoulders like a late summer shower. He just kept moving.

He was a busy man.

32

Up the Creek

The fridge came at him next. Kelly heard the condenser roar and dropped down as a barrage of ice spikes riddled the side of the bucket truck. The next round was already chambered. He spun around on the ground and got the shotgun up.

He fired. The fridge was too big of a target to miss, but the doors were too heavily armored. The buckshot round riddled the front with pockmarks, but the fridge just chugged along like William Perry. Kelly heard another round of ice spikes loading up and looked around desperately for somewhere to take cover, but he was totally exposed. The fridge had him dead to rights.

Three massive reports suddenly exploded like thunder... and the floating fridge began to list to the side like an ocean liner drifting off course.

Another thunderclap boomed, and the refrigerator spun completely. Kelly saw that four coffee cup-sized holes had been blasted into the appliance's unprotected back panel. The inside components were screaming, and smoke billowed out as the machine crashed down and pitched over completely.

With the fridge down, Kelly finally saw Ruby. She was down on one knee, looking like she was ready to propose... except instead of an engagement ring, she had his magnum held at shoulder height in perfect form. She panted heavily as smoke rose from the barrel, but her shooting stance didn't waver.

As if she couldn't be any more perfect, Kelly thought.

The bucket truck suddenly shuddered on its axles, snapping Kelly back to reality. STVN was still pinned in the wreckage, but the machine was wrestling free and Kelly was wasting time.

He made it to the controls at the rear of the truck. A trio of simple levers and a small switch to activate them. They looked as simple as when he'd found the truck where old man Conte had left it. Once again, he was grateful he had observed the old man working in the bucket truck several days ago. It would have seemed very unlikely for him to think of the truck now if it hadn't been established then first.

Kelly turned the switch and began to work the controls. At his clumsy commands, the lift began to ascend up off the back of the truck. Kelly urged it to move faster, but the boom arm moved at the same stubborn pace as another violent shove made the truck rock on its shock absorbers.

STVN King. Not dead. Not complacent. Struggling to free itself from the wreckage.

***

Ruby didn't know what Rob was planning, but she willed him on to succeed. More than that, she wished for his safety. She had two shots left in the revolver, but there was no cause to use them yet. The last surviving demon, the fan-armed robot, and Jean had fallen into a tangled battle. Saul and the alpha Rape Monster were at each other's throats again. It would appear they had a convenient bubble of time for Kelly to carry out his plan without interruption.

"Ruby..."

Ruby nearly squeezed the trigger and wasted a bullet on thin air.

She heard it again. "Ruby..."

There, sprawled on the ground in a pond of his own blood, Dr. Campbell reached up toward her. His legs were hopelessly twisted. His back had been ripped open down to the bone. But he was still hanging on. Both to life and to the bloody notebook sheets clutched in one gnarled hand.

He tried to speak again, but the strain was too much. He beckoned her closer.

Ruby got down on her knees. She took the pages from him and pressed her ear close to his lips.

"Tell me," she urged. "Tell me what to do."

***

At last, the boom was all the way up, high as Kelly wanted it. Just then, the bucket truck didn't just rock but actually *screeched* as the massive vehicle slid backward. It moved far enough for STVN's head and shoulders to squirm out and lock eyes with Kelly. The computer was no longer focused on healing. Half its face was still melted down to the black carbon-fiber skull. Its deformed mouth was twisted into a permanent black sneer. The machine's metallic black-and-gold eyes focused on Kelly's badge.

"Badge number 19," it said. "Deputy Robert Brian Kelly. Modified duty after being found indirectly responsible for the death of twelve orphans and fifteen puppies. Multiple psychiatric prescriptions."

Kelly's hand moved from one lever to another. The bucket arm swiveled at his command

STVN pressed again on the truck's frame. It skidded back a little farther.

"No wife. No children. Tell me, what is your purpose here?"

Kelly looked into STVN's black-and-gold eyes. "...Just doing my job," he said.

Kelly pulled the lever.

High above, the bucket lift swung to the left.

Straight into the power lines.

The boom arm tugged the electric cable down like an errant laundry line. The twin cables fell in a shower of sparks. Kelly leaped away, just as the lines fell atop the metal truck and the electric current ran through the chassis, through the engine block... and then enough electrical current to power the whole block ran right into STVN King's body.

The lights in the buildings around them flickered and died. In the darkness of night, the arcing lightning stood out like Fourth of July fireworks. Crackling bolts of electricity surged the length of the bucket truck and slammed into STVN's body like a pack of hunting dogs swarming a fox.

The machine screeched like a radio channel drowned in static. Its mouth yawed wide, and blue sparks stuttered inside of it. STVN spasmed and seizured. The stench of burning plastic blanketed the fairway as the machine's skin turned black and then charred like a burger left on the grill too long. It arched its back and loosed one final death cry, a warbling moan like a telephone left off the hook too long, and then slumped down.

Exhilarated, Kelly stepped back and watched the computer burn. "...Consider yourself charged," he said.

God, he loved being a cop.

***

Saul watched this scene unfold, not without some amusement. The constable had actually managed to dismantle the mechanical rival. That left only the mongrel, and some flea-bitten welp with a hard-on was hardly a challenge for a warlock of Saul's prestige.

Speaking of the beast, Saul felt fingers curl around his ankle. He looked down, and speak of the devil, there was the mutt.

Jack Wilde was flat on his stomach. The Rape Monster bled freely from a dozen wounds. One eye was sealed shut with an ugly burn. The creature's massive erection had dwindled to a pitiful half chub. There were levels to these things, and the sad truth was that the warlock was simply at a higher tier than a rabid dog with an oversized lady tickler.

That didn't change the fact that Jack Wilde meant to fight until the end.

It was a request Saul Tigges was all too happy to oblige. He reached down and grasped the Rape Monster by its blue mohawk and hauled the creature up until they were eye to eye. Jack snarled and tried to snap out and bite the warlock's face off.

Saul took advantage of the opportunity and shoved his fist into the creature's open mouth.

The Rape Monster gagged as the clenched arm forced its way down his throat. Jack bit down on the invading extremity, but the fangs gnawing at Saul's knuckles were no more bothersome than dandelion fluff. The warlock was more focused on seizing the beast's writhing tongue in the clenched trap of his fist. He squeezed, feeling the slimy muscle writhe helplessly in his grasp.

"There we are," Saul crooned.

***

On the other side of the battlefield, Jean may have been a newborn Rape Monster, but she was a fully-matured, seasoned 1980s material girl, and she didn't take shit from anyone.

She had taken some damage, a missing ear and several broken ribs, but this battle was ending one way and one way only- Jean standing tall with a Snake Demon's throat in one hand and a desk lamp neck in the other. She had battled both Saul's demon and STVN's machine until they kneeled before her, broken and powerless to stop the final coup de grace.

Jean snarled. She tightened her grip on both sets of necks. She braced herself, and then howled to the moon as she pistoned her arms up and decapitated the snake demon and the vacuum robot in a single spray of sparks and viscera.

Jean howled again and raised her arms high, glistening bones and sparking wires dangling from the severed neck stumps in her clenched claws. She looked to the alpha to share in her triumph, but Jean's victory cry turned into a wail of distress as she saw Jack down on his knees with that demon-fuck's fist rammed down his throat!

***

"I would say you've been licked, old boy." He pulled at Jack's Wilde tongue until it threatened to tear out at the root. "It's alright if you shed tear. I'll wipe it off with your-"

Another brute reeking of animal musk and ball juice slammed into him. Jack's tongue ripped like an old piece of jerky, but Saul was still tumbling to the ground with another mangy beast squatting on his chest. He caught a glimpse of yellow fangs diving toward him. Saul got his arm up just in time; the creature getting a mouth full of his forearm instead of his throat.

Not Jack! Jean snarled in her mind. She mauled the warlock's arms and shoulders. Her tent-spike claws quested for his eyes.

Her teeth were still in his arm. Saul reached up with his free hand and locked her neck in his crushing grasp. He squeezed until her trachea creaked.

NO! Jean raged. She struggled, but Saul's grip was like being caught in a car compactor. *NO!*

Yes. Saul flipped her with ease, and suddenly Jean was the one on her back, with Saul on top. The warlock's dead-slug face and glowing red eyes loomed over. He pinned her arms down like a paper doll about to be colored red all over. He grinned. Jean snapped at him, but Saul was faster, pulling his head back from her brutal jaws.

"Did you really think I'd leave myself open like that?" he asked.

And then Jack Wilde roared and rose up behind him. It was too late to do anything about it, but Saul suddenly realized the position he was in. Bent over on all fours, his rump totally exposed.

The Rape Monster bearing down on him from behind.

But there was no stopping it now. The alpha Rape Monster grasped Saul's horns like a pair of handles. Blood from his severed tongue soaked his fur, but Jack Wilde's lion's mane of an erection was fresh as a daisy. He positioned himself and...

Jack Wilde humped. He humped the warlock until his victim's fangs rattled in his head. Saul Tigges' trousers ripped like the common pantaloons of a newspaper urchin, helpless in the face of Jack Wilde's muscular, dominating-

Jack's hips hit the peak of their arch and suddenly stopped like a truck slamming into a concrete wall. He couldn't go forward and he couldn't go backward. He was trapped as surely as if he'd stuck his monster dong in wet cement. The alpha whimpered as the hole he was ravaging suddenly squeezed tighter around his member.

Saul laughed. The warlock was the roasting marshmallow on the end of a Rape Monster stick, and he cackled long and loud. Slowly, his head twisted around a full 180 degrees, the better for him to see the stupid beast's confused, panicked expression.

"Oh, you're going to have to go much deeper than that," Saul gloated. "Here, let me show you."

The Rape Monster's body suddenly jerked forward against his own will, as if a hook had been set in the tip of his wang and given a good jerk.

It pulled again. Harder this time. Jack Wilde whined like a common golden retriever.

Jean tried to intervene, but Saul kept her pinned beneath him. She was powerless to do anything as-

Jack Wilde's pelvis *cracked*. There was no more room to go forward, but he was going forward anyway. The Rape Monster's spine screeched in protest as he was pulled inexorably deeper into Saul Tigges' nether regions. Jack's body was being bent backward as if someone were forcing the front and back covers of a really, really well-written book to touch each other.

"I know. It feels cramped now, but it's much bigger on the inside," Saul assured him.

The warlock's rump went back to slurping the Rape Monster up like a string of spaghetti. There was another *crack*. Jack's spine this time, and he howled in agony. There was no stopping what was happening. His spine was touching the backs his legs. His body had disappeared into Saul's reverse gullet, up to his belly button and his thighs. Jack clawed helplessly at the air, but none of it made a difference. The Rape Monster disappeared inch by inch into the hind quarters of Saul Tigges, subsumed slowly like a boa constrictor swallowing its prey. His chest... his neck... his head.

By the end, only the tips of Jack Wilde's claws were still visible, the appendages twisted in the air as if he was waving everyone good bye.

And then, with a final *slurp*, he was gone.

Jean howled mournfully, but Saul just stood up with a loud sigh. His head rotated back around to face front. He looked down at Jean, and pinned her throat beneath the weight of one foot.

"Room for one more," he told her.

33

IF YOU SPEAK IT, THEY WILL COME

SAUL SURVEYED THE LAST of the wild mutts, the beast writhing beneath his foot like the worm it was. The Rape Monster's greenish skin had turned an ugly shade of stale peas as Saul's sole crushed the breath from her throat. The flagstaff of her erection had shriveled down mere inches. The stupid beast was moments from death.

Saul removed his foot moments before the light vanished completely from her eyes. Jean rolled over, sucking breath in through broken fangs.

Saul's actions might have been construed as sympathy for a beast that shared the same blood as his host flesh, but the truth was far from it. He simply wished to inflict more suffering on the meddlesome beast before allowing it to die.

He didn't want to actually dirty his hands on her tangled fur though, so he adjusted by willing the creature up with a wave of his hand. The Rape Monster hung in the air, suspended by invisible spider webs, as Saul considered the best way to snuff out the brute.

"What am I to do with you?" he mused.

Jean didn't respond. She couldn't. The last surviving Rape Monster floated as if she was light as a feather, but her powerful limbs felt heavy as oak trees. There was nothing she could do except hover helplessly as the red-eyed little shit with her brother's face cackled at her weakness.

***

For his own part, Kelly had been unable to move through this entire tableau.

In his defense, it was fairly difficult to do anything but stand by and watch as a sex-crime monster got sucked dick-first up the chimney of a ten-year-old possessed by a demonic warlock.

But whatever else she might be, Jean was Ruby's daughter. He shouldered the shotgun and aimed for Saul's center mass. His finger tightened on the trigger-

But Saul swayed on his feet and took a trembling step off center before Kelly could fire. As the deputy watched, the warlock shook his horned head, trying to shake off some invisible interference. Jean slipped from his mental grasp as he did. The Rape Monster collapsed in a heap, panting for breath, and Saul Tigges reeled like a drunk. Black sweat beaded on his skin. His hands began to shake uncontrollably.

The sensation was worse in his head. Saul's brain felt like it was boiling. It was almost impossible to formulate a thought through the hot bubbles churning within his skull. *What is this?* he managed to articulate. *What's happening to me?*

***

From across the fairway, Ruby's heart surged. *It's working!* she thrilled, but she quickly squelched the thought down. Dr. Campbell was barely hanging on, and his instructions were barely a whisper.

"I call on The White!" Ruby shouted. She'd been reciting the mantra for endless minutes, but it felt different in that moment. Ruby felt a new strength surging through her. Her bones thrummed with it. The effect was only growing stronger.

"I call upon the Turtle of Enormous Girth!" she cried. "And I summon the Sentinel of Manhattan!"

Ruby chanted on, feeling the forces gather around her. The energy of sheer, radiating goodness was there, massaging her shoulders and giving her a reassuring pat on the butt.

She listened carefully to Dr. Campbell's whispers, and amplified them out with all the strength she could muster. "I seek the knowledge of every wise master of the arcane who explained the forces of darkness! I ask to wield the inner strength of every woman whose weak husband was ripe for exploitation by the forces of darkness! I pray for the faith of every doubting priest who returned to the Word of God!"

In the sky high above, Saul's red stars were fading to pink. The warlock had sank down to one knee. His body wilted.

"The courage of every boy who came of age against evil!" Ruby cried. "And dogs! Dogs in general! All dogs everywhere!"

***

Kelly watched Ruby stand as tall and true as the Statue of Liberty. He stood in awe as she battered the warlock who'd stolen her son with the ringing force of every righteous and true entity. Saul Tigges' tremendous strength was running out of him like the dregs from a tap at the end of the night. He was wilting beneath the sheer power channeling out past Ruby's epic rack and through her plush lips.

It was evident that Ruby had the warlock on the ropes, but Kelly was still a gentleman. He figured a chest full of buckshot wouldn't hurt the situation.

The truck engine backfired before Kelly could pull the trigger.

Corrosive dread burning away the hope he'd felt moments ago, Kelly turned toward the bucket truck just as the tailpipe blasted off another burst of smoke and the truck engine, without the benefit of a driver to turn the key, revved to life with an ugly bellow.

The gear shift must have worked by itself as well. Kelly watched the truck drag itself away from the wall where it had pinned the computerized abomination in place. Broken parts screeching across the concrete, the truck reversed itself all the way down the street, revealing the still-standing ruins of STVN King in all his terrible glory.

The computer's skin had melted into a misshapen mass, an action figure some disturbed kid had thrown onto the barbecue. STVN grinned at Kelly, its teeth like rows of blackened charcoal briquettes.

"Other leading batteries can't last," STVN said. "But I just keep going... and going..."

It began to lurch forward, dragging itself towards the deputy once again.

Kelly watched STVN King advance. Perhaps the smart thing to do would be to run, but Ruby finally had Saul Tigges on the ropes. Might finally get her son back even. Maybe even her daughter.

If Kelly loved her, and he did love her, then the only thing he could do was buy her the time she needed.

Kelly stood his ground and shouldered the shotgun.

At least I can keep this bastard out of the picture.

He fired and hit STVN King square in the chest, blasting off the charred layer of flesh like the crust off a grill, revealing the blackened chrome of the ribs underneath.

Ruby heard the blast. Her chant broke off as she saw Kelly standing his ground and STVN shambling towards him.

"Rob!" she yelled.

Kelly heard her voice. It hit like a dagger in his back, but he didn't dare turn around. He fired another worthless blast at STVN's crusted exterior.

"Don't worry about me, Ruby! You have to finish it! For your son!"

***

Ruby's skin crawled like it was trying to jump in three directions at once. She saw Jean, her beautiful daughter even in this monstrous form. She saw Kelly, alone against the monstrous figure of her husband.

And she saw the only one she could maybe, *maybe*, do something to help- her little boy under that gravel skin and horns.

"Rubbyyy."

That was Dr. Campbell. Fading fast, but holding on for her sake. "Ruby, you have to finish it," he implored.

In her heart, she sent one last arrow of love to Robert Kelly, and then bent back closer to Dr. Campbell's pale mouth. "I'm here. Let's keep going."

34

Hands Across Mount Rape Monster

Kelly heard Ruby's voice again, firm and clear. His Ruby, even if only for a night.

"Honest farmers, men of the earth! Wrap me in your strength like a chambray work shirt!"

Not Ruby King. Not Ruby Queen. Ruby Kelly.

She could do it. He knew she could. She just needed time.

Kelly could get her that.

He pulled the trigger, but there was no burst of gunpowder. No powerful thump against his shoulder. Nothing but the empty click of a losing slot machine.

The machine heard it. STVN's clenched, skeletal teeth couldn't smile, but Kelly felt the satisfaction in the computer's relentless march toward him.

Kelly reversed his grip on the shotgun, holding it like a baseball bat, but he knew it wouldn't do any good. He might as well be offering the robotic thing a toothpick to clear its teeth once it finished chewing him up.

But there has to be something, damnit! There was a trick here. A secret weakness that could be exploited. Something you had to squint to see from a distance, but when it got close enough it was as plain as the nose on your face. The machine would grab him by the neck, and in that moment, the computer's unexpected, somewhat ironic vulnerability would pop into Kelly's head, and he would triumph over STVN King at the last possible minute.

But there wasn't. STVN didn't grab him by the neck. It molted one arm into a long nightmare-black samurai sword and stabbed it through Kelly's neck. The blade severed his spine. Arterial blood jetted out like twin elephant tusks. Death came rushing at Kelly like the crowd after the gates opened for Judas Priest, and he only had time for two thoughts before death trampled him.

The first was, *I shouldn't have used all my smarts on that "charged" line.*

The last was, *I love you, Ruby.*

And then that was end of watch for Deputy Rob Kelly.

***

Ruby saw Kelly's death from the corner of her eye. She was grateful it was at least quiet when it happened. The grief was there, but it was more manageable in her eyes than her ears.

She needed her ears. Dr. Campbell words were as much blood as breath now. She had to strain for every syllable.

But it was *working*. Saul's skin was mixed with white like dirty snow. His horns looked brittle, and his eyes were dimming like the numbers on a clock radio in need of new batteries. The warlock was reeling and clutching at empty air. The forces swirling through Ruby were driving Saul away.

My son is coming back, she promised herself.

She heard the next stanza and screamed it out into the night.

"I am the mother of the flesh that was taken, and I call your power together!" she howled. "And with this final word, I deny this interloper and cast him back to his exile!"

She bent toward Dr. Campbell again, praying that he was still holding on, but she didn't have to worry. His eyes had the same eager intensity hers did. He wanted to finish this too. The professor spat blood, cleared his throat, and lost a tooth.

Except that was wrong. The tooth wasn't lost. It was crawling up along his cheek, skittering along on long nerve endings as if they were insect legs. The root of the tooth led the way, the twin points looking like the pincers on an ant.

Dr. Campbell saw the revulsion in Ruby's eyes, but there was only confusion in his own expression. He didn't know what was crawling on his cheek. Had no idea what was happening... until the tooth bit into his cheek with its shiny new pincers.

He screamed.

They both did.

As Dr. Campbell screamed, more teeth came crawling out of his mouth.

They came as a skittering horde, yellow like unpopped popcorn kernels. An army of teeth with scissoring pincers to puncture his eyes and snip little pieces of flesh from his cheeks and his nose. Dr. Campbell shrieked as they swarmed his face in a writhing, living mass.

"Dr. Campell!" Ruby cried. "Dr. Campbell, the ritual! I can't finish it without you! Dr. Campbell, *please!*"

It was no good. Dr. Campbell tried to raise his arms, and perhaps that effort was what drained the last life out of him. He whimpered one last time, and his body seemed to deflate a little as his head slumped down and lay still.

Ruby shook him regardless. *No, not now!*

"Dr. Campbell, we're so close!" she cried. "How does it end!? What's the last word!?"

There was no response, nothing except for more blood flowing from his face and down over his gums. No noise except for the relentless teeth munching into the dead man's face.

"...That was certainly closer than I would have liked. Apparently the mother's blood cuts both ways. I should have thought of that."

Saul Tigges straightened his back and looked at Ruby with terrible lucidity. His skin was rotted grey once again. His eyes flared brightly and his horns had hardened to their former glory. Saul examined Dr. Campbell's teeth, still squirming merrily on his face.

"Actually, I'd only tried to melt his mouth shut. This... this is far more interesting."

He was distracted then by a sound like a sack of laundry hitting the ground. Laundry that was actually the mortal remains of Deputy Robert Kelly.

STVN King was on the move, lurching toward Saul again. Its blade arm dripped with blood. Its eyes crackled with charging lightning.

Saul sighed. Red light pulsed from his clenched fists as he readied another conjuration, but suddenly the whole business struck him as exhausting. Whatever energy powered the computerized thing, all of Saul's most powerful spells seemed to slide off it like a bare foot on a wet river rock. Jean was rising up too, fur standing up like dandelion fluff and hackles pulled back away from a full mouth of fangs. He reflected that even this flesh-and-blood beast with her overgrown flagpole was frustratingly difficult to keep down.

The red energy in Saul's fists slowly disappeared. The warlock opened his hands instead and let them hang loosely at his side.

"This is all starting to seem like a waste, isn't it?" he asked.

...Slowly, STVN came to a halt. The lightning faded from its eyes, but the gold circuits in its gaze ran laps as its brain ran the calculations. "It does appear that we have a 75% chance of a prolonged stalemate," it said. "Perhaps the only winning move in this game is not to play. This unit can still achieve a highly optimized state without your energy signature."

Saul allowed himself a small smile, pleased to see the machine thinking the same thing he was. "And whatever interference that's preventing me from my own full power shouldn't be an issue with enough distance between us. It's a large planet after all, we could split it at the equator."

Jean snarled, and Saul favored her with a magnanimous bow. "And, of course, Mount Rape Monster would be left as a preserve for our dear friend here."

The Rape Monster didn't relax completely, but the curtain of her lips closed over the mouth of fangs. Her tail slowly swung back and forth.

STVN King, too, seemed amenable. Its blade arm reformed into a skeletal fist.

"And what about Ruby?" it asked. "It seems we all have a claim to her."

Saul already had an answer for that too. It was time to show his own teeth.

"...Well, at least in my culture, it's customary for allies to cement their relationship with a shared meal."

He began to laugh. Jean joined in with a cackle like a hyena.

After a moment, STVN's metal jaw dropped open.

"Ha. Ha ha ha."

The triangle of eyes, red, gold, and green, turned away from each other.

And toward Ruby.

35

The End of the World as We Know It

A deep, full body chill ran over Ruby. Worse than the wet t-shirt contest she won at nineteen.

They were coming toward her now, ambling along slowly because they had all the time in the world. The warlock who'd possessed her son. Her daughter, who'd turned into a monster. Her husband who had been taken over by an evil computer program. She saw the hunger for her in all of their eyes.

Ruby took a trembling step back, for all the good it did. They matched her pace and exceeded it.

She was scared. Oh God, she was so scared. There was nothing to hold onto. Nothing in her hands and nothing in her mind.

This can't be happening, that was the thought running constantly in her vapor-locked mind. It couldn't end like this. She had done everything right.

Another step back for her. Another step closer for them.

Ruby and her friends had found all the answers. They had made a plan to defeat the forces that had decimated her family.

Another step.

She had been scared then, but there had always been hope. She knew that, somehow, things would be okay.

Then she tripped over Robert Kelly's dead body. She didn't even realize it until she was tumbling down and the asphalt was rushing up to meet her.

This is it. This is when I wake up.

But all she did was hit the rubble-strewn ground and scrape the hell out of her long torso and well-formed ass.

Saul, STVN, and Jean never gave her a chance to get back up. They swarmed around her from all sides. There was nowhere for her to turn without something horrible leering to fill her vision. Saul, forking his black tongue. STVN, who reeked of burnt plastic. Jean, foaming at the mouth.

She felt their hands on her body, each touch carrying its own terrible, unique signature: hard metal, soft, rotting flesh, wiry fur. They ripped at her clothes, revealing her lush, naked body.

Ruby screamed. She tried desperately to writhe away, but the disgusting creatures were holding her down as they continued to plunder her flesh with their hands.

And, the whole time, they were chanting her name.

"Ruby."

"Ruby."

"RUBY!"

It wasn't just the Rape Monster now. They all had their dongs out. None of them could compare to Jean's massive tenderloin, but Saul's wang was like a rotting trout with something green and rotten oozing from the end. And STVN King's ebony-chrome pecker was fully automated. It simultaneously whirred like a power drill and jackhammered at the air with devastating force.

"RUBY!"

"RUBY!"

"Oh my GOD!" she shrieked. She screamed like she was trying to let the pressure out of a tank about to explode, but it was no good. There was too much terror inside of her, and it was building faster than she could evacuate it.

"RUBY!"

"RUBY!"

"RUBY!"

36
Same as It Ever Was

It was quiet night. Oyinkan Due, better known as Oyin to her friends and simply Oh No! to those with the misfortune to work for her, was honestly a little disappointed.

Oyin was Deputy Director of Nursing. She rarely did floor inspections anymore, and she only worked nights once in, ha ha, a blue moon. Truthfully, she could spend entire weeks without leaving her office in the north wing if she so chose.

But Oyin had come up the old-fashioned way. She'd worked nights. She'd worked Christmases. She'd worked doubles and gone four weeks at a clip without a day off. She'd experienced everything there was to experience in this profession, and she had seen many an administrator become as useless as hydroxychlorquine during a pandemic because they let themselves get too separated from the people actually doing the work.

That was why Oyin still checked the leave request forms every month and personally covered a shift or two, enough to make sure she was still in touch with the reality of the job.

So, if she was going to make the effort at the advanced age of sixty-three, was a little excitement too much to ask for?

Perhaps that was why Oyin rounded the corner and shouted, "Hey! You!" a little more forcefully than she needed to.

The poor kid, barely out of high school judging by the acne shadows on his face, nearly jumped out of his hospital shoes.

"You're not supposed to be here at this hour," she said. She lowered her voice, the closest she could come to an apology, but she was damn sure going to find out what the hell was going on.

Oyin got closer and saw that the young man was an orderly and not a nurse. Technically outside her jurisdiction, but that didn't matter. If Director Hendrix was the velvet glove who shook hands with donors, Deputy Director Oh No! was the iron fist who kept the hospital running.

"Turndown was finished an hour ago. What are you still doing here?"

The skinny kid, *Paul Malerman* on his ID badge, just stuttered. "I wasn't- I forgot my-"

Oyin held up a hand, cutting off his blubbering. She realized what room they were standing in front of, and suddenly everything was clear.

"Bit old for you, isn't she?" Oyin asked.

Dark shadows of blush spread across Malerman's cheeks. His head ducked down as if offering his neck for the short, stout woman to hack it off.

Oyin, who was not quite the battleaxe her reputation made her out to be, gestured for the young man to join her at the vision panel cut into the door. "I understand. Everyone wants to look at a celebrity. But *one* look. Is that clear?"

Malerman nodded exuberantly and joined her at the glass insert.

"Doesn't look like much, does she?" Oyin asked.

Paul thought that was a little unfair. For a sixty-whatever-year-old with close-cropped lesbian hair, you could certainly tell that there'd been a lot going on there at one point. If nothing else, you could look at the generous mountain range tenting out the front of her hospital gown and conclude that she'd been absolutely fuckin' stacked back in her prime.

Of course, all of that was before you considered the matching clots of scar tissues where her eyes were supposed to be.

"Is she asleep?" Malerman asked.

"Hard to tell when she's on her back like this," Oyin replied. "She could be asleep, or she could be wide awake and playing whatever movies she plays behind those burnt-shut eyes."

"I heard she did it to herself," he asked hesitantly. He knew Deputy Director Due's reputation, but the vibe seemed to suggest she was okay. "Is that true?"

She arched a dark eyebrow at him. "You want the real truth? What actually happened and not the stories they pass around in the halls?"

Malerman nodded. "Yes, ma'am."

"Do you read, young man? Books, I mean. Fiction?"

His silence was answer enough. Oyin struggled not to roll her eyes. Gen Z. He probably had his iPhone tucked in one scrub pocket even though they weren't allowed on the floor.

"What about horror movies? Do you like those?"

He answered a bit more readily this time. "Yeah, I like those okay. *Jigsaw*. *Five Nights at Freddy's*."

"Well," Oyin pressed on. "Back in the eighties, horror novels were having a moment. I'm sure even you know who Stephen King and Dean Koontz are."

"Dean who?"

Oyin said a silent prayer. If it wasn't in an app, it might as well be hieroglyphics for these kids. "The point is that horror fiction was as popular then as TikTok is now. There were authors putting out books that sold millions of copies a month. And where there are sharks, there are always little fishies trailing along, looking for scraps. All kinds of small publishers sprung up, looking to cash in on America's sudden need to be scared. You might say they weren't too concerned about quality. The more important thing was seeing how quickly you could slap a skeleton on the cover and get a book on the shelves."

Oyin nodded at the woman lying there behind the glass.

"She worked as an editorial assistant for a two-bit operation called Gazelle Books. Kind of a quiet, mousy girl by what the police said. I see your face, young man, and don't act so surprised. Not everyone whose got it wants to flaunt it."

Malerman had the decency to blush again. Oyin continued with her tale.

"Her primary job was reading submissions. Day in and day out, reading every wannabe author's misspelled, cliche-ridden shot at being one of the titans of horror. Her editor had her working weekends and nights, but she never said a peep. Just sat there in her little cubicle, reading book after book about werewolves, slashers, and whatever other monstrosities these little ghouls could dream up. Hours upon hours. No Christmas. No Fourth of July."

"But she lost her job?" Paul asked.

"Not alone," Oyin said. "It was a layoff. All booms must come to a whimper, and 1989 was when the horror boom started to quiet down. The little shops were shutting down, and Gazelle Books was one of them. Two dozen people were told that their services would no longer be required..."

Oyin sighed.

"But Ruby King was the only one who showed up to their last day of work with a meat cleaver."

And here was the part Paul Malerman knew. The broad strokes at least. Oyin didn't keep him waiting.

"She walked into the chief editor's office while his coffee was still hot and chopped him into pieces before the cup was cold. The office had a glass front, and everybody got a front row seat as Ruby started swinging. Nobody stopped her. The best anyone managed to do was put in a call to the cops before running for the elevators.

"This was Times Square in the eighties," Oyin continued. "By the time the NYPD showed up, the editor was littered up and down 42nd street. Ruby had smashed a window open and thrown the chopped-up parts of his body as far afield as she could. The man's hacked-off wedding bells flew through an open taxi window and hit a cabbie square in the face. He veered off course and flattened a family of tourists from the Midwest. No survivors."

Paul Malerman looked a little queasy, but he didn't ask her to stop.

"Eventually, the cops made it up to the office. When they did, they found that Ruby King had gotten into the editor's cigar drawer. She'd lit a pair of stogies and stubbed them out on her own eyes. Burned them right out of her head."

"And they sent her here?" Paul asked.

Oyin nodded. "The trial was a formality. Sane people could chop their boss into pieces, sure, but they don't burn their own eyes shut when they're done. Plus, she was totally non-responsive. Near as anyone can figure, the last time Ruby King spoke to anyone was when she walked down to the corner store by her apartment and asked how much the meat cleaver cost."

Oyin looked through the window again. If Ruby King knew anyone was talking about her, she didn't show it. The old woman stayed exactly where she was, flat on her back, looking up at a ceiling that she couldn't see.

"The judge sent her here, and that's where the story gets boring. Ruby King has never responded to treatment. Never so much as whispered at any of the hotshot shrinks who thought they could make a name for themselves by curing her. She gets up. She lays down. She'll eat if you shovel it in her mouth for her, but that's it. That's been the story for the last thirty-five years."

Paul laughed. "Too many horror stories, I guess."

Oyin didn't laugh, but she did swat him lightly on his tight little butt, an HR violation that Oyin gambled the boy wouldn't bring up. "But that's the last horror story for tonight. Back down to wherever you're supposed to be," she admonished.

Paul Malerman didn't object. He didn't say anything at all, but he ventured a last shy smile at Deputy Director Due before he disappeared around the corner with his laundry basket.

Oyin finished the last of her rounds without incident, and she filed her report as such.

There was nothing out of the ordinary to report at the David J. Schow Hospital for the Criminally Insane.

37

Scenes From St. Elsewhere

Oyin was still thinking about her encounter with Paul Malerman when she returned to the night duty desk, far smaller and shabbier than the oak slab of a desk waiting for her in her regular office. She made a note to do something about that. There was no way to spread out all of the necessary reporting on this cafeteria tray of a work surface.

Ruby King had been here almost as long as Oyin had. She had been even more intensely scrutinized then, but as the years went by, the Gazelle Books Killer had turned into more of a backroom curiosity. Paul was the first person to gawk at her in a long time.

"Too many horror stories." That was what the boy had said. Oyin had let it go but, in her heart of hearts where all nurses played doctor, she wasn't so sure. She sat there in the three a.m. silence and thought about drunks who sat there guzzling Rolling Rock for twelve hours, but god help you if you had to be the one to announce that it was closing time and the taps were closed.

She wondered if maybe the problem hadn't been that Ruby King had read too many stories about possessed children and evil super computers. Maybe the problem was that Ruby had been told the tap was being cut off. Maybe Ruby didn't have to go home, but she couldn't stay here. And maybe Ruby hadn't known how to deal with that.

It was bullshit to speculate. The only person who knew what Ruby King wanted was Ruby King, and for the last thirty-six years, Ruby had been happy to do nothing but live in the world behind her burnt-out eyeballs.

But Oyin had a library of her own, and it was populated with dozens of pulpy books with skeleton covers and title fonts in dripping blood letters. *The Terror of This. The Nightmare of That.* Oyin had carried some of those books with her since they were brand new in the golden age of the '80s. Others had been painstakingly scavenged over the years from thrift shops and used book stores all up and down the east coast. Books with wrinkled spines and mustard stains on the pages. Books that creaked under the weights of the busty vampires and sadistic torturers crowding their voluminous pages. Oyin had read each of her treasures multiple times over the decades, and she knew how she would feel if somebody took them away from her.

Maybe the problem wasn't that Ruby had read too many horror books. Maybe the problem was that she hadn't read enough.

Or who the hell knew? Oyinkan Due didn't have any special inside knowledge.

What she did have was the new Dean Koontz book loaded up on her Kindle and nothing else to do for the next two hours.

Oyin made herself comfortable... and started to read.

THE END

www.ingramcontent.com/pod-product-compliance
Lightning Source LLC
LaVergne TN
LVHW031605060526
838201LV00063B/4735